CUT ON]...

CUT ON THE BIAS

Stories about women and the
clothes they wear

✂

Edited by
Stephanie Tillotson

HONNO MODERN FICTION

Published by Honno
'Ailsa Craig', Heol y Cawl, Dinas Powys, South Glamorgan,
Wales, CF64 4AH

1 2 3 4 5 6 7 8 9 10

Published with the financial support of the Welsh Books Council.

ISBN 978-1-906784-13-3

Cover image: Getty Images
Cover design: www.giselles.co.uk
Text design: Graham Preston
Printed in Wales by Gomer

CONTENTS

INTRODUCTION

Now, once upon a time… Isn't that how all good stories begin? Once upon a time, not so long ago, in a land not very far from where you are now, there lived a dreamy little girl who loved stories. She loved stories so much that her favourite thing in the whole, wide world was books. She would remember her best stories and go out into the woods near to where she lived and play at being the characters she had met in the books. Some bright mornings she was Peter Pan, some rainy afternoons she was a witch and, as she lived in Wales, there were plenty of exciting, dark damp-filled dusks. Most of all, though, she dreamed that one day she would grow up to be Robin Hood, riding through the autumn leaves with a thunder of hooves; hiding in sun-dappled clearings; sleeping under the forest canopy, wrapped in dark night skies lit only by diamond flakes of stars. She dreamed of heroic acts, freedom and, above all, adventure. She practised walking carefully across the mulched earth floor of the wood, learning not to snap twigs under her feet; she tried to fashion a bow and arrow out of a broken branch; she even tried to build a log fire but…

I didn't grow up to be Robin Hood – but I did go on to work with actors who, like children, instinctively understand that stories are about setting and much of the fun of make-believe is to do with dressing up! It's something to do with hats and wigs and make-up and shoes and changing the handbag to get it just right... Atavistically people recognise the delight in disguise. Every one of the authors whose stories have been included in this anthology have understood that the question, *What shall I wear today?* is really, *Who shall I be today?* All these stories explore the intensely personal relationships women have with what they wear; what clothes mean to them; why women choose what they do; how they consume fashion, and the subtle and sophisticated shifts in self-perception that the simple act of dressing can represent. And all have one thing in common – they are cracking good yarns! Well-crafted, fascinating, attention-grabbing, exciting and each one told in a voice that is distinctly unique and individual to the author.

With image as the central metaphor for transformation, all these stories weave colourful pictures of humour and joy, love and friendship, illness and grief, of unfulfilled lives and ugly ducklings that discover their own ways of becoming beautiful swans. One woman asks what she should wear to meet the mother who gave her up at birth, another writes of the death of a long dead brother, a third straps on her armour to enter the professional world of politics. Then there are those stories that have fun examining our contemporary obsessions with the world of fashion, celebrity styling, make-over programmes and women's magazines. Some tales are rites of passage mapping the various stages and experiences of adult lives – a wayside bomb rips a life apart, a young adult with Down's syndrome faces the future with confidence and someone, it seems, is prepared to gamble all for *that* pair of ruby slippers. This is not a one-size-fits-all collection but a book constructed to provide something for every reader – at least, that is my hope.

Clothes are objects of beauty, woven with memories and decorated with affection for ourselves and for others. Yet we cannot deny that for women, clothes have a dark side too. In August 2007, five teenagers turned on a young couple who were just spending time together in Stubbylee Park in Lancashire. The attack was so savage that the young woman later died of her injuries. Her crime? She was dressed as 'mosher' or Goth. Non-conformity may cause violence. There are countries in our world where a woman wearing trousers is considered immodest and punishable by public flogging. Image and its implications divide us as well as creating a common bond – mods and rockers, Teddy-boys, punks and skinheads, new romantics, surfers and emos; the insignia of them and us, the SS officer and the RAF pilot; the aristocrat and the revolutionary. Clothes are often the symbols of war: of class war; of finery that flourishes in lifestyles of enforced idleness; of poverty being exploited to provide our glad rags for a pittance. If naked is the truth then clothes are lies, they are proof of guilt and shame. In mythology, Adam and Eve were naked and happy until they ate and became ashamed of their bodies. I was unhappy to read for this anthology (but unfortunately not surprised by) stories that revealed the distrust many of us still feel for our female bodies, torturing them so that they will conform to something indefinable. We cover our lack of confidence, our shyness about who we are, with soft armour, one that touches us closely, intimately, makes contact with our most sensitive parts: clothes, as we know, are sexy too.

Furthermore, we in Wales know, and only too well, that language also means identity. But be they crafted as dramatic monologues, tales of the supernatural, painful diary entries or a witty exchange of emails, all these stories shape and explore the perceived world, through a language that is continually being reinvented to describe fresh experiences. These exciting, contemporary women's voices are claiming a language of creativity as their own. They are showing how it can be dressed up or dressed down, be a necessity or a luxury, practical or visceral, sensual or cerebral, used to mask or to reveal, a liberating or limiting part of our lives. We move on from the artefacts, the dresses, the shoes, the rings, the hats that help to construct our narratives – but when all is said and done, what survive are the stories we tell.

I wish to express my gratitude to Caroline, Helena, Lesley and Fran at Honno and, as always, to Janet Thomas and Jane MacNamee for their wise words and generous support. Mainly though to Margaret, my mum, who gave hours and hours of her time to help me see this project through to completion. My heartfelt thanks, however, must go to each and every one of the women who submitted their work for inclusion in this anthology. Without them there would be no book. Finally, I would like to thank all the authors who were included, working with whom proved to be the most enjoyable part of compiling and editing *Cut on the Bias*.

Stephanie Tillotson, Aberystwyth, September 2009

CLOTHES

✂

Jenny Henn

I'm a bitter old woman. I'm not allowed to say that, am I? No. I'm a 'third ager', or a 'silver surfer', or some such rubbish. Or I'm wearing purple and trekking up Machu Picchu – Machu Picchu be buggered! I haven't got the energy to drag myself onto the Merthyr bus some days. No, I've never really been able to wear, to choose, to decide what to put on, what goes with what. I wish I were a nun, or a transvestite, they always know what to wear, don't they? They're well turned out, fair play.

I'll tell you what happened last month, my friend Cathy took me to the sale at Manettes in Merthyr and she bought bag-loads of lovely clothes, not a brack in anything and I got a skirt (one size fits all). When I got it home I asked my husband and he said it looked nice – he was watching telly at the time, but when isn't he? My friend Pam said, 'You've always been the same. You told us in school that you wanted to be like Elvis because he had stage clothes put out for him.' She remembered wrong; I wanted to *be* Elvis, dress up and shake my hips about. I wanted to dance, I wanted sex, but I didn't know it then. You see, even school uniform was a minefield; the way you wore your tam said volumes about whether you were 'with it' or not. I was without it; didn't even know what 'it' was. Found out later thanks to Paul Meredith – but that's another story.

When I was little, women my age (OAPs) wore navy or fawn when they went out, and a wrap-around pinny indoors. You can't even get fawn nowadays, it's called taupe – and what happened to donkey brown and bottle green? Like I said, don't get me started.

Clothes are confusing, too many on Monday, then nothing to wear on Tuesday. Send to the catalogue, send it back. My friend Tanya only wears black but then she's Italian, perhaps I could pretend I am too.

But what I'm going to tell you happened in 1953 and, well, something else has crossed my mind and that's the nasty craze for smock tops everybody, no, every female is wearing. Men have more sense. All the women look eight months gone, even the teenagers, but the little sods probably are – I expect I'm not supposed to say that either but when it comes to clothes I'm a bitter old woman. Like I said.

I missed out on miniskirts and maxiskirts and don't even mention hot pants. Some bloke measured out his life in coffee spoons, poor dab; I can measure mine out in jumpers and cardies 'cos I didn't know what to wear.

Well, back in 1953, we had relations in Nova Scotia and they used to send us clothes parcels and Christmas cards, done by a photographer, where they all stood round in windcheaters, plaid trousers and fixed grins, and guess where Paula and Danny's clothes ended up? Got it in one: 57 Pant y Grug Avenue. Now, I know it's cold *ar ben waun Tredegar*, but it's not in the same league as Nova Scotia. Things didn't get any better when they moved to Newfoundland either. The clothes were like insulated cardboard, stiff as frozen washing, arm movements were out of the question. A polar bear couldn't have bitten through the trousers, and they were always plaid – black, red and white – colours, Mungu pointed out kindly, that had been much favoured by that old Hitler. I got upset and refused to wear the lumber jacket meant for me, so my long-suffering mother dyed it maroon (burgundy these days) so not only was I wearing walrus-proof garments, but I smelt funny. She told me, 'The smell will wear off in the wind.' Our Stephen burst out laughing, 'She do *smell* like wind.' He then ran out and I started crying and got a slap and so did he, and my father came in from work and started on us. No telly in 1953, we made our own entertainment.

Anyway, the next year we got our parcel earlier and, to my relief and my mother's dismay, there was nothing that fitted me but it all fitted Stephen, even the lovat-green tweed cap with earflaps that made him look like a garden gnome version of Sherlock Holmes. There was brand new woollen underwear and socks seemingly fashioned out of grizzly bear hide. Stephen didn't care so long as he could play Dan Dare up the backfield with Michael Nolan (my mother discouraged this, they were Dowlais Irish). Well there were even puce and grey-striped pyjamas and a Jaeger pure-wool dressing gown. Mungu was pleased and said it was a well-known fact that George Bernard Shaw would only wear Jaeger next to his skin. I asked her how she knew; she said she'd been to a Fabian Society Summer School in Porthcawl before the war and you picked up things like that. I've just thought how much I miss them all and our funny muddled way of life and I wish…well as someone once said, 'Wish in one hand and pee in the other, and see which do get filled the first.'

By January our Stephen was bad in bed and Dr Vaughan came. Stephen had a bad throat that was all, couldn't eat, couldn't even swallow water. They took him to the isolation hospital. Mam was frantic but she said he'd be out by the weekend. He came home on the Saturday and we buried him on the Thursday. I had a day off school. Our Stephen had diphtheria and that's something else you never hear of these days either, do you, come to think of it?

In March we got a letter from our Arctic garment-wearing relatives telling us they'd now moved to Labrador and sorry they hadn't sent a Christmas card but their youngest boy, Danny, had died of diphtheria, and that was why they'd sent all his clothes. They hoped we were well.

The doctors in Pen-y-Fal mental hospital in Abergavenny were kind to my Mam. They told her it was just an awful coincidence and that you couldn't catch diphtheria off clothes, but I don't know. I read years later that white settlers killed Red Indians by giving them blankets from smallpox sufferers' beds. Like I said, I don't know.

My Dad burnt all the clothes, the smoke smelt funny. It was a dry, bright spring day but his face was all wet when he came in. He said he was sweating. I hadn't known people's eyes could sweat before then. I haven't talked about this to anybody much. So, clothes, well something to keep the cold out, something to hide behind maybe, I can't say.

Dear Joanna

✂

Hilary Cooper

From: cressida@hotmail.com   sent: 6/3/2008 11.16
To: joanna@reallifemags.com
Subject: beautiful reflection

Dear Joanna,

As a loyal fan of your 'Blissful Beauty' column, I positively devoured your 'Take a Good Look at Yourself!' feature last week. Three cheers for your most astute observation that we girls are often not at ease in our own skin. High time, I decided, to give the matter some thought.

I took your advice and stood naked in front of the mirror, ready to study my body from the feet up. What better way to learn to love the contours of your own body, indeed. You did, however, omit to mention anything about locking the bedroom door first. I was only two minutes into my familiarisation exercise when Charlie burst in, two sheets to the wind after his dinner with a client. Seeing me naked, he assumed I was only waiting for him to rugby tackle me onto the bed.

No doubt you are thinking, *what a wonderful affirmation of my naked, womanly charms.* This might have been so, but, having started, as you suggested by getting to know my feet really well, I was terribly distracted by my big toes. They are actually sprouting hairs, which are grey. Seeing them made me feel about as sexy as an old man's chin – not that Charlie noticed.

Even more aggravating, I was struck, not for the first time, by Charlie's incredibly hairy feet. They are a hundred times worse than mine, but he seems perfectly unconcerned – because he is a man. The injustice of this makes me resent him horribly, especially when I remember the beautiful crocodile-skin sandals I bought in the sale at *Feng-Shoey*. I've been saving them for my god-daughter's wedding in June, but everyone knows that croc-skin and toe-beards simply do not go! Men don't understand these things – Charlie just finds me amusing.

What shall I do, dear Joanna?

Yours, disgruntled,

Cressida

. . . .

From: joanna@reallifemags.com   sent: 9/3/2008 14.23
To: cressida@hotmail.com
Subject: RE: beautiful reflection

Dear Cressida,

I am so sorry to hear of your mishap. A lock on the bedroom door can be an asset, especially with children and inebriated partners in the house.

Sally, our skincare expert, recommends having your toes waxed. It is so much more effective than shaving, which can leave you with even uglier designer stubble!

Waxing would also work for your husband – many men are discovering the benefits of a hair-free existence nowadays. Why not book a double session and be pampered together?

Best of luck!

Joanna

. . . .

From: cressida@hotmail.com sent: 11/3/2008 18.04
To: joanna@reallifemags.com
Subject: waxing

Dear Joanna,

I took your advice and had my toes waxed. It was about as painful as childbirth and the last few hairs were so stubborn they had to be pulled out with tweezers. I screamed like a cavewoman and now my big toes are so swollen I can only wear flip-flops, which is a bit chilly in March.

Charlie watched the whole thing, then his phone rang and he had to forgo his treatment and get back to the office. The nice lady said why didn't I have my legs done as well while we were about it?

I only swore twice, and we got on quite nicely until she asked me to turn over. 'Haven't you got well-defined calf muscles?' she said, in that sugary beautician tone, which really means, 'Honey, you're deformed!'

I had no idea what she meant, until I got naked in front of the mirror again. Joanna, the horror! My calves (now covered in nasty red spots from the waxing) jut out like two joints of boiled ham. How come I haven't noticed this earlier? Now I know why I never find long boots to fit.

I am in no doubt that horse riding is responsible for my ugly deformity, but horses have always been my escape from the stresses of motherhood. I can't countenance life without them. But then, it seems I am condemned to a life of bandy-legged freakdom.

All week I have paired my flip-flops with wide-bottomed trousers and fumed about the injustice of God. How could he make horse riding so detrimental to physical normality? What on earth do I wear to the wedding now? A skirt is out of the question unless I find some extra-wide boots made for fat tree trunks like mine.

Yours exasperatedly,

Cressida

....

From: joanna@reallifemags.com   sent: 12/3/2008 17.29
To: cressida@hotmail.com
Subject: RE: waxing

My dear Cressida,

I know you will hate me for this, but do you think you could be overreacting ever so slightly? The fact that you have only just noticed your calves suggests they are perfectly acceptable. In any case, many men prefer a well-developed pair of pins to the limp, spidery legs of supermodels.

Tessa – our fashion editor – has provided a list of made-to-measure footwear manufacturers. But I do think that knee-high boots may look a little out of place with a June wedding outfit.

I suggest you apply a good-quality sunless tanner to your legs the day before the wedding, taking care to avoid streaking. This will make your legs look longer and slimmer.

And don't give up your horse riding, dear. Every mother needs her escape, especially while the children are still at home.

Always remember, beauty is more about inner calm and confidence than outward perfection.

Yours,

Joanna

....

From: cressida@hotmail.com sent: 17/3/2008 22.47
To: joanna@reallifemags.com
Subject: depression

Joanna!

I really wish you hadn't mentioned the children!

While I was hunting for fake tan in my wardrobe, I found an old picture of me in a bikini. The first thing I noticed was how little my tummy used to be. The mirror cannot lie: nowadays I have quite a paunch overhanging my knicker elastic!

This week I have done 100 sit-ups a day, before I even step out of the bedroom, but there are stretch marks and flabby skin which only the best plastic surgeon could remove.

I feel quite resentful towards Toby and Camilla for doing this to me. So resentful, in fact, that I made an appointment to discuss a post-childbirth tummy tuck with my GP. Doctor Garston was most sympathetic when I explained how I am sliding into depression, which only plastic surgery will cure.

'But, Mrs Crabbington-Fosse,' he said, with his sweet little smile, 'there isn't any provision for purely cosmetic surgery on the NHS.'

Couldn't he see that Charlie would have to get the most impossible bonus to pay for a tummy tuck and clear my credit card balance? I burst into tears.

He handed over the tissues and said, You may have a touch of Irritable Bowel Syndrome which is making you bloated. We may need to consider your diet and some exercise.

A diet! Of course, really he thinks I'm a gluttonous pig who just can't stop eating, so only a stomach staple will save me from terminal obesity. This realisation made me totally hysterical and I used up his whole box of tissues.

Poor Doctor Garston was blown away by the strength of my feelings. 'Have you thought about taking something to lighten your mood?' he said, looking very concerned.

I came away with a prescription for Prozac, which is supposed to help me forget all my physical deformities from now onwards. Charlie has made me promise never to read 'Blissful Beauty' again.

Yours, depressed,

Cressida

....

From: joanna@reallifemags.com   sent: 18/3/2008 09.07
To: cressida@hotmail.com
Subject: RE: depression

My dear Cressida,

I do feel rather concerned that looking in the mirror has left you in such a sorry state. I confess I feel quite responsible.

But do you think that the close self-examination and reflection I suggested may have been the trigger for pre-existing unresolved issues to surface? Or did you close your eyes in front of the mirror until now? Thankfully, none of my other readers have reacted quite like you. In any case, I am so glad to hear you are getting some much-needed help with your problems.

Jasmine, our alternative health expert, suggests that you try St John's Wort – a natural remedy for depression – and Oil of Evening Primrose, which promotes hormonal stability.

Yours, ever,

Joanna

....

From: cressida@hotmail.com   sent: 19/3/2008 02.38
To: joanna@reallifemags.com
Subject: old bag

Hormonal stability? I see where you are leading! You think this could all be linked to the menopause, don't you! I hadn't thought of myself as anywhere near that old yet, but I obviously sound it to you.

I sat on the end of the bed, in the bright sunlight, and took a good, hard look in the mirror. And do you know what? You were quite right – there was an old, wrinkled crone looking back at me. She has crows feet round her eyes and skin like old leather. I cried for nearly an hour, but it is better not to be self-deluded.
Of course, Charlie says I am mad – that I don't look a day over twenty-five. But he has been saying that since I was eighteen, and he has always lied to keep me happy.

I told Chrissie and Lou what you said, when we met up for lunch. They made disapproving clucking noises. Chrissie said you were being a frightful bitch and Lou said I look beautiful, but I know their game. They're secretly pleased that I'm wrinkly and overweight. Chrissie's thinking, 'Hurrah! Now I won't feel such a bloater beside her,' and Lou is sighing with relief because her Jeremy won't ogle my cleavage across the dinner table any more.

They're my best friends, but they don't want me to be slim and beautiful, actually. So now I resent them too.

Is there any hope for me? I fear not – unless Charlie's bonus is big enough to cover a tummy tuck *and* a facelift.

Yours, in the slough of despond,

Cressida

....

From: joanna@reallifemags.com   sent: 20/3/2008 18.50
To: cressida@hotmail.com
Subject: Rubbish!

Now Cressida,

I simply cannot believe this. Send me a current photograph of yourself. I have an inkling you are actually a willowy, peachy-skinned blonde who just needs her self-confidence restoring. Does that sound bitchy to you?

In the meantime, it sounds as though you are suffering from stress and need to pamper yourself a little. Try to do something every day to make yourself feel special and valued. I like to have a small glass of champagne with my breakfast, just for a treat, and as I sip it I tell myself, 'You deserve this!'

I'm sure you can find something which will do the same for you.

Joanna

....

From: cressida@hotmail.com   sent: 23/3/2008 09:24
To: joanna@reallifemags.com
Subject: whoops

Joanna,

I thought your champagne idea was absolutely wonderful. So good, in fact, that I realised I deserved more than one glass, and finished the bottle. I probably should have waited until after breakfast: the bubbles were a bit much on an empty stomach. When I went to take Toby and Camilla to school, I reversed Charlie's Audi into the gatepost.

Of course, Charlie is sulking. He says he can't believe you encourage drink-driving. Don't worry, I stopped him from calling his lawyer – it was only a crumpled wing, really – but he says there'll be no cash left for a tummy tuck now.

I enclose a recent photo of me at last year's hunt. I'm the one Prince Charles is looking at with a lascivious twinkle in his eye.

Yours, hungover,

Cressida

....

From: joanna@reallifemags.com   sent: 24/3/2008 22.13
To: cressida@hotmail.com
Subject: RE: whoops

My dear Cressida!

I am not in the least surprised that you caught the eye of our future sovereign! You led me to believe I should expect a hirsute geriatric dwarf, but this elegant horsewoman has a figure most women would kill for.

As for your beauty, your radiant smile lights up your whole face. Are you forgetting to smile, dear? Because that could be making you feel less than your best.

Now go and smile at yourself in the mirror. It's all about seeing yourself as you are, you ridiculous girl!

Yours, jealously,

Joanna

PS. So sorry to hear about the car.

....

From: cressida@hotmail.com   sent: 24/3/2008 23:55
To: joanna@reallifemags.com
Subject: flatterywillgetyounowhere

Dear Joanna,

I see you homed in on my smile. No doubt you decided to overlook my chipped front tooth in your assessment. It makes me look totally goofy if I beam unreservedly, but I've learnt how to keep my top lip over the worst of it. So, the camera does lie, you see.

It also fails to capture the white stains on all my front teeth – the result of my mother going overboard with fluoride tablets when I was a child. So my mother is partly to blame for my unconfident smile.

The fact that she was not there when Pru Lumley cracked my front tooth with her lacrosse stick, does nothing to temper the simmering resentment I now feel towards her.

Yours, unconvinced,

Cressida

....

From: joanna@reallifemags.com   sent: 25/3/2008 02.08
To: cressida@hotmail.com
Subject: somepeople

Dear Cressida,

I think you should remove the mirror from your bedroom wall.

Loosha, our Feng shui consultant, suggests replacing the mirror with a picture which makes you feel calm and happy. Try a sunny beach scene, or a tranquil mountain top. It could be somewhere you have visited, somewhere which holds happy memories for you. Take time to visualise yourself there, in that beautiful picture, and enjoy the serenity of the moment.

Best wishes, as ever,

Joanna

....

From: cressida@hotmail.com sent: 29/3/2008 05:21
To: joanna@reallifemags.com
Subject: desperation

Joanna,

I have the picture: it's a sunset between the palm trees on a tropical beach. I can hear the waves rolling onto the sand and almost taste the pina colada. (In fact, I quite often have one, just to aid the realism a bit.)

The only problem arises when I imagine myself being there. All of a sudden, a squat, wrinkled hag with deformed calves and rabbit teeth appears between the palm trees and beckons to me. I approach, full of dread, and look into her sun-frazzled face. Then I realise this hideous relic of womanhood is actually me.

Usually, that's when I wake up screaming. I've been having the most terrible nightmares and I may need to go back to the doctor for sleeping pills.

Any more clever suggestions??

Cressida

....

From: joanna@reallifemags.com sent: 29/3/2008 05.22
To: cressida@hotmail.com
Subject: Out of office reply

Hello and thank you for your message.

This auto-response is just to let you know I am out of the office for the next two weeks while I am on holiday.

Please contact Julie, our features editor, with any urgent requests, or you can leave a message for me to pick up when I return.

Best wishes and stay beautiful!

Joanna

....

From: cressida@hotmail.com   sent: 30/3/2008 10:19
To: joanna@reallifemags.com
Subject: Holidays

Joanna,

What a coincidence! Yes, I know you won't get this until you return, but I just had to share the good news. I shall be out of the office too, in a manner of speaking. Charlie thinks I need some time away and has booked me into the Still Waters clinic for some good old TLC. I'm hoping to see someone famous – I hear all the celebrities go there to get over their cocaine addiction.

I do hope you are having a wonderful holiday. I'm trying not to feel jealous of you, looking slinky and tanned in your designer swimsuit, somewhere on a sun-kissed beach. No doubt the local male population will be swooning over you – I hope it isn't too arduous fending them off.

Cressida

....

From: cressida@hotmail.com   sent: 15/4/2008 16:54
To: joanna@reallifemags.com
Subject: friendly advice

Well! What a colossal surprise! I could hardly believe it was you at the clinic.

Wasn't it lucky the nurse called out your name just as I walked past? Otherwise I would never have realised it was you. You don't look a bit like your picture in the magazine. I expect it was taken years ago – and those black and white photos disguise age wonderfully, don't they.

I wondered whether they had you on some sort of medication which might have unpleasant side effects? That glazed expression and the lank, greasy hair surely can't be normal for a successful journalist. You would think that, in such a celebrity-friendly clinic, they'd let you see a hairdresser to keep your roots up to scratch.

To tell you the truth, Joanna, I thought you looked pretty awful. You've clearly been under a lot of strain lately. I assume that's why you were chain-smoking, but no good will come of it, you know. You've obviously done the right thing, putting yourself in the hands of the professionals.

What a shame we only got chance for the one little chat. The nurse said you were too poorly to come out of your room after that. I was hoping that, after all the kindness you've shown me, I might be able to offer you some emotional support. As a fellow sufferer, I know exactly what you are going through.

At first, I thought it incredibly rude when you said, 'You put me in here.' Then I realised that, as you once said to me, I was just the trigger which enabled your unresolved emotional issues to surface. It's nice to feel useful, isn't it.

In fact, you've helped me in so many ways. After our meeting, I looked at myself in the bathroom mirror (they wouldn't let me have one in my room) and I thought, Well, I only look half Joanna's age! That was a turning point for me, I can tell you.

I've been home nearly a week now and I'm feeling fine – especially since Charlie's bonus arrived. He's treating me to a tummy tuck at the Pouting Clinic next month.

Here's hoping you soon feel chipper again. Have you thought about a facelift, by the way? It would take years off you, dear Joanna.

Yours ever,

Cressida

....

Black Cherries

✂

Lindsay Ashford

I can never eat cherries now, although I used to love them. And I can never wear that dark berry red. The taste of cherries reminds me of Selena Jones. Cherries and red velvet. The colour and texture of death.

She came to stay with us in April 1968. I was nine years old and was just getting used to the idea of living in a hotel. Dad had almost bankrupted himself converting the place. It was a dilapidated Edwardian mansion that had once boasted an aviary, from whose broken windows the birds had long since escaped. It occupied an unenviable position on the main road between Wolverhampton and Bilston. Not a holiday destination but, with heavy industry booming in the West Midlands, there were plenty of businessmen looking for a bed for the night.

There were hardly ever any women among the guests, so Selena stood out like an exotic bloom. She was a jazz singer and had been booked to appear at one of the clubs in the town. I heard Mum telling my brother that she had never heard of her, but she was, nonetheless, slightly star-struck when Selena stepped out of the taxi.

I thought she was the tallest person I had ever seen, although she was probably about the same height as my dad. The gold slingback stilettos and backcombed hair must have added a good six inches. She wore tight black slacks and a fur jacket that was almost the same colour as her skin. As she signed the guests' book Mum whispered to me that it was mink.

I suppose her eyes could have been described as sultry, their impact heightened by the way she had of looking at you with the lids half-closed. Her lips were full and wide and her teeth whiter-than-white but it was her hands that I most remember. That first day she returned from a trip to the shops with a bulging paper bag. She came into the kitchen – which all the guests seemed to do sooner or later even though they weren't supposed to – and sat down at the table. Her long brown fingers delved into the bag and pulled something out. Reaching across, she popped it into my mouth, telling me to make sure I didn't swallow the stone.

I remember the sweetness on my tongue and the juice running down my chin. She wiped it with a tissue then fed me another one. And another. Her nails were painted the same dark red as the cherries and the movement of her fingers from the bag to my mouth was hypnotic. My trance-like state was broken by Mum coming into the room, saying something about cherries being out of season and wanting to know where Selena had found them.

With hindsight I was clearly a child who craved attention and most of the time my parents were too busy to give it. You might call it a crush; I suppose that's what it was. But if Selena had me under her spell it wasn't long before the rest of the family followed suit.

That evening, when Selena had gone to the club, Mum took me up to her room to sneak a look at the dresses. Her excitement was contagious. As she slid back the wardrobe door she gave a little gasp. Pearl-encrusted oyster satin fought for space with sparkling silver lurex and black silk trimmed with feathers. A backless gown of turquoise lace rubbed up against a sequinned catsuit with batwing sleeves. But the one Mum pulled out – the one she held up against herself in front of the mirror – was a velvet gown with what looked like strings of diamonds for straps. The dress was the colour of Selena's fingernails.

'Frank Usher,' Mum breathed, peering at the label. 'Do you think it'd suit me?' She smiled as she said it, so I knew she was joking. I smiled back, relieved that she wasn't expecting an answer. Even if she had been slim enough to fit into it I could see that the dark red would have looked awful against her pale, sun-starved skin.

My brother pulled a face when I told him what we'd done. Martin was six years older than me and had shied away from Selena's hands when she'd tried to ruffle his hair. I was pleased. I wanted her all to myself.

I was disappointed that she wasn't up and about the next morning when we had to leave for church. Mum explained that she worked late; that the club didn't shut its doors until two in the morning and Selena would need a lie-in. I remember Dad nodding and saying something about keeping her away from the other guests. He didn't come to church with us but that was nothing new. I think Mum only went because my brother was in the choir and she liked to see him in his cassock and surplice.

I liked the smell of church but the services bored me so much I spent most of the time watching people in the pews, making up names for them and imagining them doing embarrassing things like picking their noses or going to the loo. There was a pale, gaunt-looking man who Mum had often pointed out to me. 'There's Enoch,' she'd whisper, in a voice as reverent as the one she used for the Lord's Prayer. I had no idea who Enoch was. I knew he was something to do with the government but at nine years old politics was a word I barely understood. On that particular Sunday, though, Enoch imprinted himself on my mind in a way that I and everyone else in the congregation would never forget. When the service was over and everyone was filing out we found our way blocked by a gang of men with notepads and cameras.

'Tell us what you think of niggers, Enoch!' one of them shouted.

'Are you going to resign, Mr Powell?' another called out.

'What's going on, Mum?' I tugged at her sleeve, frightened by the tone of their voices even though I didn't understand what they were doing.

'It's nothing,' she said, her voice high and shrill. 'Come on – let's get you home.'

'You're a wicked man, Enoch! I don't know how you've got the brass neck to go inside that church!' A woman's voice this time.

As the accusations flew, a man I recognised squeezed out from somewhere behind us. It was Mr Williams, the butcher who delivered meat to the hotel. 'It needed saying!' he shouted, his right hand punching the air. 'Enoch's right! Send 'em all home, I say!'

Suddenly everyone was yelling. Men and women. Even some of the choirboys. As I covered my ears I saw Enoch slip away down the steps at the side of the porch. Two of the men who gave out the prayer books went with him. Flashes of light and the whirr of cameras followed us as we followed Enoch. Finally, from the safety of Mum's Hillman Minx, we watched as he was whisked away.

Mum didn't say a word on the drive home, apart from hissing at us to shush in the back. Martin was teasing me, asking if I knew what a nigger was. I did know. I'd heard it at school. Andrew Jarvis used to shout it at Jennifer Samuels if she skipped too close to the piles of pullovers the boys used for goalposts.

'Selena Jones is a nigger,' Martin whispered, 'and Enoch's going to send her home!'

I poked him hard in the ribs, willing Mum to drive faster. When we got home I ran into the dining room, hoping to find Selena having breakfast. But she wasn't there. She wasn't in the kitchen either. I scurried off to find Dad, demanding to know where she'd gone. He gave me a funny little smile and said she wasn't up yet. He said I could take a pot of coffee and the newspaper up to her room if I liked.

As he folded the newspaper to put it on the tray I caught sight of a photo of the man in church. Beside the picture, in big letters, were the words: 'Rivers of Blood'. I wanted to ask Dad what it meant but he was holding the kitchen door open, waiting for me to take the tray. 'Go on,' he said, 'or the coffee'll get cold.'

Selena smiled when she saw me standing outside her room. She beckoned me in and patted the bed, piling up pillows so I could sit beside her. Her eyes looked different. Smaller. When

I said so she laughed and pointed at a little plastic container on the dressing table. I had never seen false eyelashes before and she showed me the tiny tube of glue she used to stick them on. I asked if she would stick them on me and she reached for the newspaper, spreading it out to catch the lashes in case they fell onto the bed. I saw her eyes cloud when she saw the headline.

'What does it mean?' I watched her cherry-coloured nails fiddle with the glue tube, not daring to look up at her face. I was afraid she would shout, like the people outside church.

'Rivers of Blood,' she muttered, squirting a thin white line along the black spidery thing resting in her palm. 'The man's a menace.'

I told her what I'd seen that morning; about the butcher and the men with cameras. 'But not everyone's like that,' she whispered, pressing the false lash onto my eyelid. 'Your mum and dad – they're not like that, are they?'

'No,' I murmured, remembering the way Mum had said Enoch's name.

My eyes felt itchy when I came down the stairs. I'd wanted to keep the lashes on to show Mum but Selena said she might not approve and that it should be our secret. I liked that. As I made my way down the passageway to the kitchen I could hear Mum and Dad talking.

'Good old Enoch!' That was him.

'I could have killed those bloody reporters – they know he's right.' That was her.

I darted away, through the side door that led to my bedroom. I crawled under the bed, pulling the fringed candlewick down to the floor to make a dark, safe hiding place. I growled into the carpet that I hated them both and I never wanted to speak to them again.

They were so busy with lunches and dinners that day that I don't think they even noticed how angry I was. That night, as I lay in bed, I heard Selena getting ready to go to the club. I imagined her looking through her wardrobe, deciding which dress to wear. How I wished she could take me with her, away from my rotten parents into a world full of sequins and false eyelashes.

The movements stopped and I heard the door close. Selena had gone. I must have dozed off for a while but I woke up suddenly. I could hear the creaking of floorboards overhead. Good, I thought, she's back. I glanced at the luminous hands of the clock beside the bed. Half past eleven. It couldn't be her – Mum said the club didn't close until two o'clock. In my sleep-fuddled state I decided that burglars might be trying to steal her dresses. I had to go and investigate.

The door to Mum and Dad's room was open and I could see Mum's head above the bedclothes, fast asleep. Dad wasn't there. He usually stayed in the bar until the last of the guests went to bed. I crept past Martin's door, which was shut, and made for the staircase. I don't know what the male guests would have said if they'd seen a nine-year-old in a nightdress wandering along the landing but luckily I didn't bump into any of them. I made a detour to the airing cupboard, where Mum hid the master keys to the bedrooms. Then I tiptoed along the passageway that led to Selena's room.

I paused at the door, listening. I could hear the creaking again, loud and clear. I wasn't sure what I was going to do if it was a burglar but I felt an overwhelming urge to protect Selena and her dresses. Sliding the key into the lock I opened the door.

What I saw is burned into my brain. I can never forget the sight of those white shoulders, those diamond straps, that dark red velvet and my brother's face as he turned from the mirror.

'You won't tell, will you?'

I didn't tell. Not Selena, not my parents. The next day she brought me more cherries but I couldn't eat them. I told her I felt sick and she rubbed her chin with her long brown fingers, nodding as if she understood.

She left at the end of the week and no one ever mentioned her again. I tried to wipe the whole thing from my mind. In the years that followed I never attempted to speak to Martin about it – not even when he told me he was getting married.

His daughter was nine years old when they found him lying in the bath with his wrists slashed. His wife, numb with disbelief, described the scene in all its gory horror. And she showed me the note he'd left, transporting me back in time to that Sunday all those years ago. To Selena's room: to that dark red dress with the diamond straps. And the newspaper, still lying on the bed, with its awful headline.

Would things have been different if I'd told Mum and Dad about the dress? Could they have accepted Martin for what he was? Allowed his life to take a different course? I don't think so. People could be exotic, alternative, as long as they were only passing through; as long as you didn't have to live alongside them.

Martin was, like the cherries, a thing out of season. If he had been born in a different time, to different people, he might be alive still. God knows I've tortured myself over it, but I only have to look at my niece to know that whatever was wrong with Martin's life, something wonderful came out of it.

I saw a photo, years ago, of Selena. It was in a newspaper article about a gangster. It said she was his girlfriend. I don't know if it was true, but I hope that, whoever she's with, she's happy. Like all of us, she deserves to be loved.

LIFESTYLES

✂

Joanna Piesse

It was held by the Court of Appeal that if the disparate elements that go together to make up a lifestyle are sufficiently inventive and show an original creative step the lifestyle is copyright and is protected in law. **Law Society Journal, 10 June, 2014.**

'Just follow her.'

'Isn't that stalking?'

'It's research.' Kim reaches for her make-up bag in the top drawer of her desk. Her leaf-green cashmere cardigan pulls at the button at chest level. She adds a few strokes of mascara and her light hazel eyes flick to Melanie. 'Don't get followed, don't be seen. Take photos, detailed notes, routines, times, places, brands, flavours.' She checks back in the mirror, smiles and deflects the smile to Melanie.

Melanie breathes in. 'Could I talk to you about getting some of my own cases? I need to start sending out letters under my own name.'

'Your own name.' All three words are elongated through stretched lips as Kim strokes on *Claret Cream* gloss. 'I have a new client meeting then a partners' lunch.' She zips her make-up bag. 'Where did you get that outfit?'

Melanie glances down at her torso. It's a 1980s boxy black suit with a New Romantic-style blouse. 'A vintage clothing shop.'

Kim nods and moves as if to go but instead checks her watch, swivels back and taps at her keyboard. Uneven sounds of baby voices, of things being banged, of outrage, of instructions to 'share' filter into the office. She concentrates on the screen, her eyes searching. Eyes still on the screen she picks up the phone. 'Kim Greenly here. Nikita is at the playdough table again. She was there when I checked at 8.30 a.m. We agreed stimulating play, one-on-one, for two hours a day. When does that two hours start?'

Ambrose, the managing partner, puts his head round the door, a file under his arm. Kim gives her roguish smile and picks up her jacket. As she passes Melanie she smiles her chummy smile and winks a hazel eye, 'You'll be great. Have the first report on my desk when I'm back from lunch. Ambrose…'

Keeping her head down, Melanie hurries after Dawn. The low November sun is dazzling gold but without heat. Dawn moves swiftly, fur boots eating up the pavements. She reaches St James' Park and mingles with others criss-crossing the park to assignations or meetings. Melanie's leather-soled shoes are slippery on the fine film of ice. Dawn's phone rings, she stops and turns, frowning into it. Melanie, in pursuit, is stranded on the bridge; she takes out her phone and fiddles with it, tourist-style. The government buildings could almost be the Kremlin in the gilding light; she zaps a couple of pictures.

She watches a woman her own age, with a briefcase, walk purposefully towards Horse Guards Parade. She could ask for a transfer to another department: conveyancing; wills; matrimonial; something with face-to-face meetings and her own clients. Melanie's ears and nose begin to lose sensation; it feels like the process of becoming invisible. She looks at the birds scratching around the lake before raising her eyes to scan the park. Dawn is moving fast towards the St James area.

When Melanie sat scribbling endless notes in tort and contract lectures this was not how she imagined her first job as a trainee solicitor. She wanted to work in the copyright field and thought of herself fighting the corner of an author who'd lived for a year on soup and carrots to finance the writing of a novel, only to find it ripped off. She couldn't believe it when she'd landed a job with Barber and Willis. She began to see herself wrestling pirates in the music industry and shaking Madonna's hand. She imagined conferences in Europe discussing the difficulties of protection in the climate of the digital revolution.

On Melanie's first day in the office she had been the envy of male and female trainees – she was to work for Kim Greenly. Her job: to assist at the cutting edge of Kim's boutique practice in lifestyle cases.

In 2014 the court held that a person's lifestyle could, if it were sufficiently inventive and comprised an original creative step, be copyright. The first case was that of *Beady v Lincoln*. The original step was the way the plaintiff had so fully woven aspects of the East Anglian coastline into her life and philosophy. Her clothes and house and jewellery were the greys and blues of the coast, she invented recipes using samphire and developed a form of meditation based on high-flying wheeling gulls. When a visiting tourist returned to London and opened a highly successful relaxation centre using the new form of meditation and launched a clothing line using greys and blues and featuring driftwood, top London copyright solicitor Kim Greenly was engaged to fight the groundbreaking case. The claim was that an original lifestyle had been copied, and exploited. The plaintiff received substantial damages and Kim Greenly notched up the ladder from salaried to equity partner. Since then celebrities and leaders of fashion began to eye each other more keenly than ever.

In the case Melanie is working on, the person marketing herself as Dawn is thought to be copying the lifestyle of a successful Russian business woman. Melanie has followed Dawn into a Polish café and watches her. Melanie hates these cases; they make her feel as if she is erasing herself at the same time as trying to capture someone else. Dawn talks animatedly with the café owner over shots of vodka. Melanie huddles in a corner and taps notes into her BlackBerry®, she smiles as she does so and gives the occasional snort of laughter, as though texting a friend. 'Grey fur hat. Fur boots. Wrap-over cardigan and scarf in plum. Gilt earrings of ornate crosses. Brooch on hat of a mini-triptych.' She switches to her flip-top phone and cups her hand partially over it as if it is a compact. She captures a picture of Dawn laughing, wearing the fur hat with one earring swinging.

There is a clatter as the waitress, clocking the photo, jolts

Melanie's beetroot soup onto the table. 'Is that everything?'

'Yes, thanks.'

The waitress begins to turn.

'No, actually, no. I know this must look strange. That's my colleague from the office over there. I think she's arranging a leaving party for my boss and I know some of the people invited are allergic to fish.'

The waitress turns back to look her full in the face.

'She's quite difficult to speak to, she thinks I'm after her job; she'll think I'm interfering.' Melanie leans closer to the waitress, 'But I am very worried about the fish issue. It's these allergies; one woman in the office only has to sniff a prawn and she's out cold.'

The waitress's mouth is a moue of disbelief.

Melanie folds some sour cream into her soup, watching the white streaks appear. 'Okay. This is the deal.' She looks up at the waitress, 'I want to know if she is arranging a business-type lunch, if so, is it fish and if it is, which fish?'

'Which. Fish.' The waitress' voice is flatter than a lemon sole.

Melanie slides a £20 note towards her. It lies on the table between them; beats pass. Melanie adds an identical note and tastes her soup.

The notes are palmed from the table. The waitress saunters over to wipe varnished tables near Dawn and the café owner.

Melanie watches the three of them. This is the third lifestyle case she has worked on. Most of the clients are women, all accusing each other in the 'you've-copied-off-me' way of the playground. The legal protection of lifestyles has pushed merchandising on a stage for celebrities. You can buy a 'Katie

Price relaxing weekend break' in a cardboard box; it comes with a pot of the correct type of face cream, details of bedtime routines with the kids and a tape for the daily workout. You can buy the itinerary of a day's shopping trip with Victoria Beckham, drink the same coffee, sing the same song in the car, visit the same shops. The singer Angel Ravine is trailing a promotion for how she winds down after concerts which includes the design of her tracksuit.

The waitress returns. 'It is a fish lunch, "Fish from the Baltic". Doesn't sound like a leaving-do to me. They're going to call it "Baltic Beauties" or something.'

'Thank you.'

The waitress' eyes travel deliberately over Melanie, taking in the dark wool pelt of the business coat, giving Melanie time to colour. 'And she doesn't look like your colleague.'

'Good.' Kim speed reads the report.

Melanie wonders how it is that Kim always smells slightly of sex, even under the Chanel fragrance.

'Good lunch?'

'Mmm. Oysters.' Kim riffles through the attached receipts and photos. 'The client whose lifestyle is being copied by Dawn is coming in for a meeting first thing tomorrow morning. Get out there and see if you can get any more on Dawn.' Kim gets out her mirror.

'I think she saw me in the café, she'll recognise me.'

'No one has so far.' Kim flips a look up and down Melanie, then wipes a little grease from the corner of her lips.

'There's the report from the private eye.'

'Men don't get these cases, they can't spot the earring or the way the scarf is worn. I want fresh information.' Kim's eyes dart to her screen and she picks up the phone on its first ring. 'Kim Greenly... Sky News? All matters relating to my clients are subject to client confidentiality. Just a comment...yes...of course... This is the first potential case based on a man. The copyright position could be different as it involves the Royal family.' She replaces the phone and looks Melanie full in the face. 'Someone has appeared at three events dressed in precisely the same clothes, and carrying the same accessories, as King William.'

'Kim, I've never followed anyone twice in one day, wearing the same clothes.'

'King William! I have a meeting tomorrow. There will be an updated report on my desk.'

'Let me have this file. My client.'

'No one will notice you, Melanie.' Kim's fingers begin to tap the phone under her hand. 'I'm writing your trainee report this week.' She grimaces a tooth-white smile of dismissal and her hand flexes on the phone.

As Melanie is on her way out of the door a voice comes from behind her. 'Where did you say that vintage clothing shop is?'

File Note: *Aurora Dmitrievna Stakhanov. New client of Kim Greenly. Based in Moscow. Aurora is active in design and fashion world in Moscow, draws heavily on Russian Orthodox influence. Has lines in jewellery and wedding outfits. Developed anti-ageing diet of North Sea fish, popularised by regular public lunches for women in Moscow over past three years. Wears fur. Is putting together fragrance based on smell of birch tree forest. Practises a* *form of meditation involving Russian orthodox chants. Meeting arranged with Kim Greenly, Wed 18th Nov, to discuss suspected lifestyle infringement by woman operating in London, known as Dawn.*

Melanie waits for two hours outside the deli, knowing that Dawn often stops here on her way home. Bottled cherries, rye bread, tinned fish and a jar of organic honey. Dawn reaches to get something extra from the dairy counter. Melanie can't quite see what, a container of some sort, a green swirl on the lid. She mustn't miss it. She gets closer, 'S' something, her eyes scan the shelves. Soured cream. Good. Melanie picks up a tub and puts it in her basket, joining the bottled cherries, rye bread, tinned fish and honey she has already picked up, imitating Dawn.

Melanie will dump the food as soon as she has paid for it and has the receipt for evidence of lifestyle infringement to go on the file. The first time she was sent shadow shopping she crammed the food into her briefcase and ate it that evening. But in the night the case went round and round in her head and she woke, bloated and confused.

Outside the shop Melanie lowers the shopping into a waste bin, her shoulders tense. There is likely to be CCTV coverage around here and she imagines being stopped by a bulky police officer at the next corner and questioned about possible terrorist activities.

She hurries after Dawn on her numb feet. She turns the corner.

Dawn is waiting, gloved hands on hips. 'Are you a journalist?'

'No. Yes.'

'I've seen you before. Who do you work for?'

'Er, *Your Style* magazine. We're doing a feature on fur and the fashion industry.'

Dawn looks Melanie up and down. 'I don't think so.'

'I happened to notice your hat. Is it arctic fox? Perhaps we could arrange an interview?'

As Dawn leans in Melanie focuses on large pores clogged with make-up. The smell of perfume and foundation is mingled. 'Creep. Stay away from me.'

Kim is at her desk when Melanie arrives with the report at 8.30 a.m. Kim is wearing a 1980s boxy black suit and a New Romantic-style blouse. Something about it is all wrong. The white frill on the collar makes her look, how does it make her look? Like a piece of meat on a plate.

'She recognised me.'

'What?' Kim clasps her hand to her mouth and runs out.

Melanie opens a file on her computer. She makes brief notes about what she was wearing yesterday and what Kim is wearing today. She times and dates the file note. The note is headed *Melanie v Kim – Lifestyle Infringement date ???*

When Kim is settled back behind her desk Melanie decides the blouse makes Kim resemble a Dutch still life painting. A fish perhaps with a glassy eye and a sheeny greenish skin; the grey filing cabinets behind her are the pewter background. 'You look terrible. Sort of shiny.'

'Bloody oysters.' Kim lurches away from her computer towards the door again, past Melanie. 'Up all night.'

In the air behind her she leaves pockets of sour breath

hanging, as if too many people have been breathing the same air. From her computer webcam link comes the sound of children fighting over the playdough.

While Kim is away from her desk Melanie takes two calls. The first is from Sky News. They have a live piece to camera on the Royal story at 9 a.m. They have a comment from the Palace and Elton John is linked up to the studio to give the celebrity angle. They want a discussion in the studio between a leading psychologist who treats celebrities and Kim Greenly, and to include Elton on the link-up. The second call announces that the Russian client is in reception.

The colour rushes back into Kim's face when Melanie tells her of the first call. 'What did you tell them? How do I look? Are they sending a cab?'

'You'd look better if you borrowed my earrings and shoes.'

Kim begins to toss off her shoes.

'I'll go ahead with the meeting with Aurora then.'

'You've got to stand in the front line sometime, Melanie, get on with it. What about my hair?'

Kim steams off wearing Melanie's shoes and earrings. Melanie opens her computer file and makes some more notes.

Reception was filled with the light heady smell of birch trees and the aureole of a fur hat. Melanie greeted Aurora and explained Kim's absence. Over coffee and pastries Melanie presented her research and went through recent case law and the possibilities of action and settlement. Aurora pressed an invitation on Melanie to visit her in Moscow, or to stay at her dacha at any time.

In the afternoon Melanie got a call from Ambrose's PA to say he was in back-to-back meetings all day but maybe they could meet the next day for a light salad lunch to discuss her Russian case.

The nursery called for Kim to say Nikita was covered in an angry rash and must be picked up immediately. After checking the webcam for proof of spots, Kim left in a flurry of files and barked instructions to patch calls through to her. The office fell silent. Melanie drifted over to Kim's desk and was able simply to lift the phone when the call came through from William Windsor. An infectious disease she explained, no proper diagnosis yet, one can't be too careful. She would, she said, be only too happy; she knew all there was to know about 'Lifestyle' cases. After replacing the phone she opened Kim's desk drawer, took out Kim's mirror and lipstick and stroked the *Claret Cream* gloss over her lips, smiling at her reflection.

Mr Price's Summer Holiday

✄

Alys Conran

Whoopeeeeeee! Naked! A comedy of bodies with dangly bits, breasts reaching down and hanging genitals. Pubic hair gathers in knots between legs all across the beach, sometimes rising in a big black bush, curls tight, sometimes wavy, golden under the sun, warm ambers in places, a fuzziness of autumn. And then there's the shaved: grainy under the sun, pubes like iron filings. Across the beach, legs and arms swarm like sausages, curling over each other against the sand. A girl, a redhead, pretty, stretches her arms behind her head, yawning, boobs to the air. 'Ahhh,' she says, happily. Her companion, dark haired and more bashful, giggles, wriggling a dip in the sand with her legs.

Further up the beach, Mr Price, a new arrival, adjusts his sinking backside on the towel. (The towel will have puckered his arse cheeks, dammit. Hard work this naturism. Hard bloody work.) He lies back on the sand, tries to enjoy the sun's rays: *Caressing your naked body* the website had said. Mr Price had thought *that* sounded lovely. He could do with a bit of a caress.

But, thing is, will his testicles burn? He has no idea if it is *done* to smother the genitals in sun cream. Exposed to the eyes of those two youthful, nubile bodies he's just spotted nearby, can he casually reach for the yellow bottle? Pour the white cream into his hand? And spread a thin layer over his most sensitive parts?

No, he cannot, definitely not.

Can he ask them for help? Mr Price contemplates this possibility fondly for a moment, watching the fragments of them that are in his line of vision; a smooth shoulder, the mound of a breast, a jutting hip languishing on the towel. Then, remembering where he is, and that every bodily urge will be publicly witnessed, he thinks hard about Mrs Brown, the dinner lady at the school where he works, until his naked body is obediently unenthused again and he can lie back, flaccid against the sand.

The two young girls continue to soak it up, boobs eyeing the sky.

'D'you reckon this is normal over here?' says the redhead to the brunette, still with her arms behind her head.

'Yeah, probly.'

'Yeah. They're so much more liberal. Not like us. *God* – we even get embarrassed when *kids* run round naked.'

'Yeah.'

'I mean – it's sick. What's wrong with us? It's all that TV and magazines, makes us think we should look a certain way, not have lumps and bumps, be flat and thin like models. I mean, who decides what we should look like?'

'Yeah, dunno.'

'Anywayz, I feel good. It's so much better like this, don't you reckon?'

'Yeah, totally.'

'I mean, what's the point in a bikini? Three little triangles of material... stupid idea.'

'Yeah, pathetic.'

'I mean, why be embarrassed about what we are? Right?'

'Right.'

'Clothes are just a *social convention* anyway.'

'Yeah.'

'Can you put some cream on my back so I can turn over?'

'Yeah, sure.'

Mr Price tries not to watch as the dark-haired girl lifts her body from the towel, her black hair falling in twists down her back, tries to pull his eyes away from that back as she kneels, her round behind resting neatly against her feet as she starts to squirt the white cream onto the redhead's smooth body, tries not to stare as her hands work down her friend's back, or when the other girl takes over lower down, to smear the cream round and round her own buttocks until they glisten under the sun. Mr Price sits up to hide his shame.

The girls have run out of cream. The brunette's back shudders as she hits at the plastic bottle, teasing out the last few drops. Half grateful for this technical hitch in his peepshow, Mr Price pulls his eyes away from them to watch one of the Latin

American salesmen trudging along the beach, fully clothed, pedalling fizzy drinks and slices of coconut to the sunbathers, who ignore him with disdain and irritation. Beyond him, the blue Mediterranean licks invitingly at the beach and a few tousled bathers splash around, blissful in the shallows.

Once the girls are safely lying on their fronts, lithe backs to the air, Mr Price decides to give his smarting testicles a dip. Hoping that his behind is neither too mottled by the towel nor too white, Mr Price pushes himself to his feet, and, although the effort is lost on their basking backs, saunters casually past the girls and into the sea. Ahhhhh!

Delicious coolness. In the clear blue water, self-consciousness receding from him with the shoreline, Mr Price frolics around, swims under water, and lies with his head back, his feet pointing out of the sea, and his little naked toes twinkling. How sweet! How heavenly! How free! Now Mr Price is truly relaxed. For at least the next ten minutes.

His body growing cold, Mr Price starts to wonder how to make his exit. He looks up to the beach beyond the water and the shapes of those two bodies, now lying on their backs, magazines and arms shielding their faces from the sun. The cool sea will have depleted the impression he will make upon leaving the water, *that* is inevitable. But…just do it. That's the thing. Just *do* it.

Three seconds later, Mr Price is wading in the shallows, the water streaming off his naked body, the wet drips seeming to flee him in this moment of need. He swings his arms with determined abandon, heading straight up the beach toward the girls. Closing on them, until he can make out the nail varnish on their toes, the line of one girl's jaw – the rest of the face still shadowed by the clean angle of an arm – Mr Price feels a sense of tremendous happiness and health, freedom, and joyful pride. Mr Price, walking tall, squaring his shoulders, already feeling a little bronzed after all, is preparing his lines, working out the fine details of them:

- *Hi, girls.* No, no way.
- *Hey, you two.* Better.
- *I see you need some more cream.* No!
- *D'you need some more sun block?* An improvement.

Three metres or so away now and Mr Price is ready, is starting to grin in exhilaration, his smile winning and broad. Feeling suddenly virile, wild, and exotic in his nakedness, he is just about to make his presence known, when, just then, the redhead sits up and pushes her hair from her face. Seeing Mr Price, she cocks her head to one side and leans back on her arms to observe him lazily.

Mr Price stops, intimidated. The girl, without taking her eyes from Mr Price, pats her companion's thigh so that the brunette pulls the magazine from across her face and pushes herself to a sitting position, bringing her knees to her chest as a barrier. They both stare at him, their eyes wandering irreverently up and down the length of his body, their faces expressionless.

Mr Price's pre-prepared lines flitter out of his mind.

'…Erm… hello?' he says.

The hello drifts up and across the beach, empty, inarticulate, inappropriate. Mr Price, sucking in his soft belly tissue, tries to regain some of his stature, to muster the dregs of that manly well-being, drained away by the eyes of these two.

'Hi,' says the redhead, her voice flat.

'H…having a…nice time?' Says Mr Price, cold, trembling, dripping-wet: a schoolteacher, middle-aged.

'Yep. You?' The girl's irises seem empty – unflinching, like the barrel of a gun, and, for Mr Price, the long corridors and smart teenaged retorts of term time are suddenly laced with sweetness – the refuge of a comprehensive, the shelter of his desk, the exquisite imperfections of year nine's homework, of year eleven's failed exams, suddenly all as enticing as Page Three.

'L…lovely…thanks. Lovely. Yes, lovely. Ha ha…nice change.'

'Hmm,' the redhead eyes him with suspicious disdain. The brunette looks to her companion, her nose crinkling in distaste.

'A…anyway…' Mr Price is hopeful still, as if waiting for the lottery numbers. 'I err…was wondering if you…girls need ah…anything. Anything at all…erm like, erm, cream, maybe?'

'Oh, God,' mutters the redhead to her companion, who crinkles a nostril, raises her eyebrows, and, nodding in agreement, says, 'Yeah, *God,*' emphatically too.

Mr Price, his ambitions shrinking to a cold shudder, tries to regain a little of the face he's lost.

'…only I noticed, you girls had…run out.'

'Well we haven't, it's fine,' says the redhead.

'Yeah, we're fine,' says the brunette.

'Oh…good. Good! That's a relief!' says Mr Price '…only, you see… I know how terrible it is to get a sunburn…*awful.*'

'So I see,' says the redhead motioning to Mr Price's nether regions. Her companion begins to giggle.

Mr Price looks down, sees his white feet, his hairy, pale legs, his thighs, a kind of peach off-white, and then the angry red circle of sunburn around his groin, spreading to around five inches from his genitals, the whole area he had designated too private for public application. Mr Price fidgets to cover the flaming skin with the only thing available to him – his hands. Harshly aware of his pallid skin, his red cheeks, his concave chest and his spindly legs, Mr Price backs away; feels the blue sea behind him, aching to take him in again.

The redhead watches him, a hazy smile spreading across her face, a strand of hair falling across her forehead. Then seeming to get an idea, she springs to her feet.

'So, you want to help us to apply it?' she asks, smiling like Hollywood, her hand playing in her luscious hair, her breasts jutting at the bare sky, and her toe poking at the hot sand beneath it all. Behind the magnificent figure she cuts, the brunette giggles like a gremlin.

'No...my God no!' says Mr Price thinking Mrs Brown, Mrs Brown, Mrs Brown, even as words dribble in desperation from his quivering mouth.

'No! I...erm...was concerned about your skin...yes...the effects of the sun...can be v...very dangerous...'

The redhead walks slowly toward Mr Price, swaying her hips, like something from one of the adverts.

Mr Price, never having found himself in such a fortuitous situation, is suddenly terrified. The redhead keeps walking, smiling at him, and Mr Price starts to feel dizzy with fear. The redhead, raising one seductive eyebrow, her mouth curling at the edges like a tigress, is reaching out a long beautiful arm to touch Mr Price's hot cheek and, at the shock of her touch, Mr Price, hitherto too stunned to move a muscle, springs into action.

Mr Price's hands cup around his red crotch as he backs off, scuttling backward across the beach away from the aggressor. 'Anyway…the cream's there if you want it…lovely weather! Nice change! Yes, very nice. Lovely. Ho ho…yes…' His voice rises to an emasculated treble clef as he cowers, beating a stuttering retreat.

The girl snorts, first a covert giggle, and then a full belly laugh, her hands on her hips and her head thrown back with the mirth, and the brunette joins in as Mr Price shuffles backward into the sea, sweating, muttering pleasantries, clutching at himself and at decorum, before finally turning in desperation and, with a small leap, so that his white and pink, corned beef buttocks lift somewhat gracefully into the air, he dives beneath the waves, the girls' laughter pealing behind him like the howls of wolves.

'Ugh! Did you see his legs?' says the redhead through her laughter.

'Yeah, gross!'

'I mean he was old enough to be our dad.'

'*Yeah…*sick!'

As Mr Price swims away, they settle back down on their towels and take up their magazines – where airbrushed beauties strike their habitual poses, sleek against the glossy pages.

'Ah well… ten more minutes and I'm done…you?'

'Yeah, cool.'

A few minutes later, as they pull on their thongs, wriggle into their skintight jeans, don their push-up bras and designer glasses, roll up their towels into their black leather shoulder bags, and rearrange their hair, the redhead reflects—

'It's been good though, don't you reckon? So many people just happy to be starkers! Not like the lemmings at home.'

'Yeah, totally.'

'At home, everyone just thinks the same way. Know what I mean?'

'Yeah…yeah—'

They trudge on up the beach beneath a waning sun, dangling patent sandals from their long fingers and disappear into a beachfront café full of freshly bronzed young talent, to wash down their day in the sun with long glasses of sangria and chit-chat laced with spite.

And, even as the sun tracks a slow descent across the glassy sky, Mr Price still swims, naked and terrified, far out in the Mediterranean, the people on the beach just toy-sized peachy figures in the distance. So that it is only later, much later, in the dusk of early evening, that Mr Price will finally come to land, shivering and dripping his exhausted way up the beach, to depart the resort in a chaos of Y-fronts and socks, trousers and long, modest, teacherly sleeves frantically reclaimed.

BACK TO BLACK

✂

Carys Green

After you'd gone, I fell back to black. Alone for the first time in seven years. I felt uncomfortably exposed, going round the supermarket with a basket instead of a trolley, looking at the meals for one. I decided I wasn't very hungry after all. So I hid. In black.

Black is slimming. Though I'm slimmer than ever now. Without even trying I've lost twenty pounds, and I can honestly say I never felt hungry. Never.

Black is safe. Just like you made me feel safe…at what point did I stop feeling safe? Was it when I wore red to your brother's wedding?

The first time I planned to leave, you found out and locked me in the bathroom for nine-and-a-half hours. Of course you were full of 'sorrys' and 'fresh starts'. You told me to dress up and you'd take me down the club for dinner and a dance. Like we used to.

The second time you'd gone to Ireland for the rugby and I had a head start. I emptied the airing cupboard into a suitcase and called a taxi. I spent hours dragging the kids round town with the number of the women's refuge scribbled on my palm. The wheel of the suitcase had long since fallen off by the time I reached the safe house. It was dark. All I can remember was opening that bloody case to get the kids' pyjamas, and sobbing, as all I'd packed was towels, towels, a pillowcase and duvet set, and more towels.

I had to borrow clothes left behind by the other women. There were bin bags in the attic, mostly full of kids' stuff. The few items that fitted belonged to a woman who'd just left.

So, for a week, I dressed as Hilda. Hilda had seven children, with names like Summer and Leaf and Sky, who never went to school. One of the other women, who remembered her, told me Hilda didn't want to live in a house; she wanted a cave, or a tree or a yurt by a stream. Social services were forever hounding her. Wherever she is, I wish her well and thank her for the jingly-jangly skirt made from old saris, the tie-dyed t-shirts and the batik dress with moons and stars.

Hilda did not wear shoes – and I'd left in a pair of slippers. So, with the change from the taxi and twenty Silk Cut, I went into Primark and picked up a pair of flip-flops and some underwear for the kids.

There is something very temporary about flip-flops. Something almost throw-away. They get left on the beach, too close to the tide. The toe-strap breaks halfway round Tesco's. They are not built to last – especially the pretty ones with sparkly straps and patterned soles.

Nor was my new life built to last. I don't know how you

found me, but you did. I got in the car with you. Just to talk. You sped off before I could secure my seat belt – then slammed down the brakes on the dual carriageway. I lost a front tooth when my face met the dashboard—

After a while I ceased to care about my appearance. Everything I wore was wrong. I was a skinny cow. I looked like a tart. The years faded by, as I did, in my jeans and jogging bottoms.

When I heard about the accident at Fiveways, I cried for hours. Days. Weeks. People knew. People knew what went on. I did the right thing. I fell back to black. I cleared out your cupboards of jeans, jumpers, rugby tops and a suit that never did fit.

After you'd gone I fell back to black. But it's not you I'm mourning; it's all the reasons I was with you in the first place. It's a lifetime lost to low self-esteem and loose-fit leggings. It's not you I'm mourning – it's who I am.

When I have finished mourning I will be able to look myself in the mirror. I will be able to see in colour.

When will that be?

I don't know, but I'm guessing that an intensive course of retail therapy might help me get there!

THE LUCKY JACKET

Yasmin Ali

She had enough to worry about without this. Rufus was at a difficult age, the *Daily Mail* was giving her a hard time over the Obesity White Paper, and there were rumours of a plot by that bastard at the Home Office. The last thing Julia Carrington needed was the coffee stain on her pale wool jacket. She dabbed at the dull brown mark with a towel, first moistened with a few drops of water, then dry, but if anything the stain seemed to be darkening, taking on a clearer form, like an image emerging on photographic paper.

'Shit,' muttered Julia, 'shit, shit, shit.'

Putting the jacket on for inspection in the mirror revealed the full extent of the problem. The Secretary of State's jacket was now embellished with a faux nipple in exactly the spot where the real one might be.

'Shireen!' called Julia, exiting the ministerial bathroom and activating the intercom connecting her to her diary secretary.

'You do have a spare suit in the office, Minister. More than one. Would you like me to get them?' Shireen was a briskly efficient woman who ensured her ministers were always prepared for any eventuality.

'I know that,' snapped Julia, 'but the press conference this afternoon—' The hint of querulousness in the minister's voice was barely detectable, but Shireen was attuned to her boss in ways which transcended Civil Service training. She reached out and took the jacket from the minister, in a move that was both brisk and solicitous.

'Leave it with me, Minister. I'll see what I can do.'

Julia Carrington slipped on another jacket before taking the stairs to the meeting room on the sixth floor. There was a private lift, but Julia was determined to maintain her elegant figure despite the sedentary lifestyle of the modern politician. Nor did she actually need to wear a jacket for the meeting with her ministerial team. The building was well heated, and the government's style was one of purposeful informality; all shirt sleeves and weekend Levis for the older men, Paul Smith suits, or even the occasional Ozwald Boateng, for the younger ones. Ties were strictly for the press corps. But Julia knew that those rules were for the guys, not for her. Leopard-print kitten heels notwithstanding, the Thatcher power suit was still de rigeur for the ladies. In any case, a policy meeting with her team was always a matinee with a pit of snakes. Julia's deputy wanted her job and was leaking to the Treasury team in a bid to get it. One of the junior ministers was a plant from the Whips' office. Even her PPS was up to something; probably pillow talk with that little fox from Sky News. Tailoring was the best body armour available to the contemporary woman politician.

Julia walked into the room attended by her Permanent Secretary and sat at the head of the table in a manner calculated to quell any residual chatter. Phil was studying his cufflinks, but if that was as close to insolence as he could manage, then Julia need not anticipate anything she couldn't handle. In any case, the secret of managing these meetings was to keep away from the abstract, the theoretical or anything moot, and, if possible, to spend so much time on matters arising from the previous meeting that there would be no time to consider any other business.

The meeting, to anyone looking in, indeed, to almost all the participants, looked to be brisk and constructive. But Julia was not quite on ministerial autopilot, despite appearances. She'd rightly assumed that none of the men, however fastidious they were about their own appearance, would notice that she was wearing a black jacket with a beige skirt and tan shoes, and as for Marion Bolton, the junior minister, the less said the better. There was a very good reason why Marion always did the radio interviews, never television. But this was a back-room meeting. The press conference in the afternoon was something else.

Press conferences are ten a penny in Whitehall. Even with something as contentious as the Obesity White Paper the most that might normally be expected was a 20 second clip on the rolling news channels. Why waste airtime on a politician when the subject gave news editors a hook upon which to hang repeat freak-show footage of Britain's fattest teenagers? Julia knew all this, and yet she also knew another truth; on live television anything can happen. The best you can do is be prepared, and that very much includes how you look.

Julia was lunching at her desk on something involving quinoa and wheat berries when her political advisor entered the room looking grave.

'We need to talk,' said Karen.

'It'll have to wait,' said Julia, barely glancing up from her laptop.

'It can't, I'm afraid. It's the *Daily Mail*.'

'There's a news conference this afternoon, can't they ask their questions then?'

'Not really,' said Karen, 'At least, it wouldn't be the best place to start. the *Mail* is planning to run a story. They'd like you to comment before they break it. It's about Phil.'

Julia's politician's reflexes were well honed. Her demeanour remained impassive as Karen began to relate the details. The Minister of State, Phil Cooper, had been filmed secretly at a private party snorting coke in the company of an under-dressed reality television celebrity.

'How long has Phil known about this? More to the point, where is he now? What's he got to say for himself?'

'He's known for about an hour, since he came out of the meeting this morning,' said Karen. 'He's been with Arvind ever since, working out a line. Arvind told me what they've got, and the *Mail* has been on to you for a statement in the last ten minutes. Number Ten's in the loop, too, but obviously they want distance.'

'It had to be a bloody health minister, didn't it?' said Julia.

'I don't know,' mused Karen, 'at least he's not in charge of policing.'

Working out a line was simple enough. Phil Cooper had worn

a sneer on his face from the time he had been appointed to the department, and lost no opportunity to try to upstage or wrong foot his boss. Julia could not resist a bat squeak of pleasure at the man's misfortune, but it was beneath her dignity to express that in any way publicly. In any case, Phil had been Number Ten's creature; gloating would look like disloyalty to the PM, and Julia was certainly not about to fall into that trap.

'Let's use this as an opportunity to convey a health message,' mused Julia. 'Something about the dangers for promising young professionals in high pressure jobs self-medicating with Class A drugs instead of striving to get their work/life balance right. Positive messages about how to handle stress at work, all that stuff. Layard's happiness agenda, you know the script.'

'Number Ten will be content with that. But we can't just issue a statement. The press conference this afternoon can't exactly be postponed, and you can be sure that there'll be much more interest in it now that there's a story for the red tops. We'll need to rehearse your responses to the questions you're bound to get.'

Julia knew all this. She was a consummate politician. Always on top of her brief, quick-thinking, and with a natural ability to walk the fine line between reason and empathy. Above all, Julia knew that most successful political careers required hard work and thorough preparation. But there was something else, too. Something Julia would never acknowledge, even to her closest confidantes. Julia was morbidly superstitious about her clothes.

Clothes, Julia knew somewhere deep within, had powers. The trouble was, there was no way of knowing what their powers might be at the point of purchase. A suit might look pure West Wing when she slipped it on in the changing room at Liberty, but it was entirely possible that it would contain the malign inclination to derail a statement in the House, or jinx a speech to the World Health Organisation. Julia had a strict rule that new clothes could not be worn for any important occasion; everything had to be tested first for signs of demonic intent, and only then could it be eased into the working wardrobe.

The even-more important rule was that when facing a significant challenge it was not enough to wear something one knew not to be cursed. It was axiomatic that some clothes were suffused with magical protective powers that could make the wearer invulnerable. Today had turned into a day that cried out for *the lucky jacket*.

The Q&A rehearsal went well enough. Karen lobbed quickfire questions, swerving abruptly between arcane details of policy, opportunist try-ons, and downright malevolent jibes at the fallen minister's inability to decline any invitation to party, no matter how unsuitable. Julia responded calmly, fluently, and with exaggerated courtesy.

'Try to vary your tone,' suggested Karen. 'Slick politicians are out of favour at the moment; everyone thinks they're spinning. Let's have a little disappointment that Phil's let us all down, the odd hesitation to show you're thinking on your feet, even a note of contrition. Contrition has been going down brilliantly with the focus groups.'

Julia nodded to indicate that she was assimilating the feedback. 'How about something like this? No one could be more disappointed than I am that one of my team has behaved in this way. I've always had the highest regard for

Phil Cooper's considerable abilities as a policymaker, but moral character matters just as much. I'm truly sorry if I've failed to communicate that to my team.'

'Yeah, sorry's good.'

'I'd better get myself ready now,' said Julia, glancing across at the clock on the wall. Once again, she pressed the buzzer that summoned her diary secretary.

Shireen entered the room carrying two suits, one navy, one red. Julia raised an eyebrow.

'I'm sorry, Minister. I had your jacket biked across to the cleaning service in Knightsbridge. If anyone can get rid of that stain, they can, but when I called them a few minutes ago they were still working on it.'

'That's all right,' Julia said, 'I know you're all doing your best.' What Julia really knew was that evil forces were waging proxy war against her by wounding her lucky jacket. She suspected that Phil had cast a spell whilst polishing his magic cufflinks. 'If he thinks he's taking me down with him—'

'I'm sorry, Minister, I didn't quite catch that,' said Shireen.

'No, I'm sorry, I'm thinking aloud.' Julia reached out a hand. 'The navy one, I think. Red might look a little frivolous in the circumstances.'

Julia was arranging her scarf before the mirror, doing her best to cajole the blameless navy suit into developing a late surge of good fortune when Karen returned to the office a little breathlessly, her BlackBerry® clutched tightly to her chest. Julia looked at her expectantly, and the expectations were not pleasant ones.

'Where's Phil? I can't go to this press conference without seeing him. I haven't even seen a draft resignation letter. What's he playing at?'

'Phil hasn't resigned yet. And the rumour is that the coke pics are just the start of the story. Apparently the party took a turn for the Max Mosleys after that.'

'Jesus Christ, Karen. Please don't tell me the papers have got a picture of a member of this government dressed as a Nazi.'

'I'd say it's more fetish than Nazi, and in any case, it's just the girls in the leather corsets. The problem is, it's a video, and the sound quality's pretty good too. He makes his opinion of you forcefully clear. You know what cokeheads are like.'

'I don't want to have to cancel this press conference. It's bad enough that the White Paper will get no attention now, but I don't want to make the political fallout from this any worse by giving the impression that the Department is in a state of panic. Have you talked to William about this? Can I talk to the PM? We've got less than an hour!'

Karen looked at her BlackBerry®. 'I've just got something from Arvind. Phil's resignation letter. It's rather terse, insolent even, and there's nothing in the way of an apology to you, but if William says Number Ten's happy with it, we may as well go with it to keep things on schedule.'

Julia was disinclined to take Karen's advice. It made sense, in terms of handling the immediate situation, but Julia knew that to take the obvious course would also be to hand Phil Cooper and his laddish cronies a delicious little victory; one that would convince them that although they'd taken casualties, they were still in with the prospect of winning the war.

'No. Tell Arvind that the letter won't do. And set up a call to the PM. This is still my Department, and I still care about my White Paper, and I'm not going to be derailed by little boys playing silly games!'

'I'll pop down to see Arvind,' Karen began.

'No you don't! Summon him up to see you. Summon him up to see you here, in my office. Sit him down on that chair, the nice, low easy chair. Then you stand up, walk over to that table and perch yourself on the edge. Tower over him, talk down to him, talk over him, don't let him get a word in edgeways. Draft the letter on the spot. I want Phil Cooper to grovel. I want him grovelling to me. Now get on with it. I'll take the PM's call in Shireen's office.'

Julia was beginning to feel that she was getting back in command of the situation. Just one thing still nagged at her. The navy suit. The skirt length was wrong; it was just a bit county lady. The jacket had strange lapels which made the slender minister look weirdly bosomy. The scarf could be arranged to disguise this, but the scarf itself was problematic, its Pucci print a distraction.

The phone rang. Shireen answered, her back almost imperceptibly straightening as she said, 'The Prime Minister for you, Minister.' With that she stood and moved silently out of the office.

In the larger office next door, Karen was treating her colleague Arvind as the junior, which, strictly speaking, he was. Seated on the low chair, papers and phones slipping from his lap, Arvind took dictation from Karen, his attempts at intervention peremptorily dismissed.

'How about, "I have greatly valued the opportunity to work for someone as dedicated and capable as the Secretary of State, and I can only regret the fact that I have been unable to match her high standards of public service, or emulate her ability to behave in private as she urges others to do as a matter of public policy."'

Julia's task of persuading the Prime Minister to support her more effectively was a tougher one than that entrusted to her assistant.

'I do think that we can turn this into an opportunity to promote a public health message, Prime Minister,' Julia began.

'If that's how you want to handle it, fine, it keeps the matter wholly within the department, which is obviously best for the government and for the party. I'll keep out of the whole business as far as possible,' he was saying, as the door to the office opened quietly, and Shireen entered, a garment bag in her hands. Shireen unzipped the bag as quietly as she could, removed the pale beige jacket, and held it up for Julia to inspect. The Prime Minister, warming to this theme, carried on talking, whilst Julia looked at the fabric under the halogen desk light, the warm side lights, and finally in the natural light that flooded through the window once the blinds had been pulled aside. Of the offending stain, no trace could be seen.

Shireen opened the door to a small walk-in wardrobe and took out a skirt to match the jacket, a crêpe de Chine shirt, and a pair of elegant Ferragamo court shoes. Julia switched the telephone to loudspeaker and continued her conversation with the Prime Minister whilst shrugging out of the matronly navy jacket, the frumpy skirt and the shiny shell top. Clad only in a surprisingly racy set of La Perla underwear, Julia took advantage of a fractional Prime Ministerial pause to interject a few thoughts of her own.

'We are in complete agreement about the best way to handle this business,' Julia began. 'The Department should and will lead, and we will put the emphasis on health education rather than accepting that it's some kind of grubby sex scandal.' Shireen held the skirt out, the waistband somewhere below knee level, and Julia stepped in with great delicacy, whereupon her assistant pulled it up to her waist and fastened the zip.

'But it would be a mistake not to take a robust line to prevent this from becoming part of a continuing narrative of sleaze.' Julia said this as she slipped her arms into the light silk blouse.

'Phil Cooper is not, alas, a one-off rogue. He has friends, back room boys, maybe, but how many of them were at this party? Or others? It's a small step from a few jokey gossip columns to an unstoppable story. I'm happy to lead on the health message, but it's in your interests and the party's that you make something of an example of Phil Cooper.'

As Julia completed her re-robing by slipping on the lucky jacket, the Prime Minister was saying, 'Yes, that is a scenario for which we ought to be prepared. I'll get William to liaise with you about the details, but I'm sure you're right on this. You have my full support.'

A short time later an assured Julia Carrington in an understated neutral suit looked out at the massed ranks of the media. Only two onlookers detected the hint of a smile being suppressed by the Minister, and only one guessed the real reason.

PLUMAGE

✂

Sarah Taylor

Jennifer eyed the pigeon as it skirted leafy puddles, tiptoeing towards the seeds she had scattered across the netting. She had watched it for days as she sat eating her lunch on the stone bench by the children's paddling pool, the park birds fluttering round the crumbs she carelessly threw towards them. This was by far the most handsome of them, silky grey feathers shading into iridescent purple around its neck. She had decided early on Tuesday that it would do very nicely indeed, and had set out for the park with her nylon trap folded into her handbag.

She lifted the roll she had brought for lunch, careful to sweep her fingers across the top so that the crust flaked out into the air. The crumbs were carried onto the path by the afternoon breeze. There were sparrows twittering in the leaves above her and there was no harm in scattering her net a little wider. Just in case.

Glancing out across the pool she saw a young family entering the park, a little girl in pink shorts and a halter-neck top tottering eagerly towards the pool. A laughing woman jogged behind her. The child reached the pool and splashed in, thrusting her hands deep into the water to scoop it out in a spray that soaked her from head to toe. The mother slowed, sat down on the stone wall of the pool and, taking a paperback from the vast bag slung over her shoulder, bent back the spine and lowered her head to read.

A sudden flutter drew Jennifer's attention back to the bird. It bobbed and wove towards her, ducking its head down to peck up the proffered seeds. She wondered why it was on its own today, why no other pigeons had joined it in the very generous lunch she had provided. She had, after all, spent an extra few pounds on the premium seed. She felt this little satin specimen was worth the investment. She didn't expect to harvest any other birds today. This was certainly the one that she wanted, but one couldn't complain about any little extra picked up along the way. Still, she thought, a bird in the hand and all that.

Behind her in the trees she heard the sparrows again, a faint fluttering, a warning sound of chirps. Did they know?

The pigeon hesitated, head cocked to one side, listening. One foot hovered over the silken trap. She held her breath. Slowly the bird lowered its foot to balance itself and, with a quick twitch of the thread, she had snared it, dragging it across the gravel towards her. Its eyes bulged with fear, wings thrashing helplessly against the ground.

She leaned forward eagerly and held the bird in her palms, feeling the frantic beating of its heart and gently stroking the beautiful glistening feathers round its neck. A quick twist and it was all over; she deftly opened her handbag and dropped the bird into a waiting handkerchief.

Only as she bent to secure the bag's clasp did she realise that the splashing had stopped. She looked up. Across the park the little girl was standing stock still in the middle of the pool, her eyes widening in horror, her mouth a perfect little shocked 'o'.

She got to her feet, hurrying to the exit. She knew it was only a matter of time.

Behind her she heard the high wail as the girl began to scream.

Back in her rooms she set out the feathers from the park bird. Sixteen perfect purple plumes, selected for their colour and shine, lay on the glass work surface in her small kitchen. She had cleaned them and carefully caressed oil into each silken tuft to protect their condition. She smiled as she carried them into her bedroom, eager to add them to her creation; it was almost complete. She opened the door, flicked the light on, and felt her heart flutter.

In the middle of the room stood a tailor's dummy: a dress hanging lightly from the torso, cinched in at the waist and sweeping to the floor.

The bodice was sparrow: speckled flecks of plumage that were soft as cashmere to the touch. Chocolate brown spotted with shimmering black. Loops of plover, interwoven with oriole, formed delicate straps over the shoulders. The oriole had added a flash of bright yellow, striking against the more muted plover. She remembered fondly the day that she had come across that particular little catch. It had cost her dear. A week's stay, high season, in the fens, sucking up to all those dreary twitchers, till one pointed out where the exquisite buttercup-and-black birds could be found.

The neck of the gown scooped down like the swoop of a kite descending on its prey. Always flat-chested, she had not been able to resist the joke of scattering great tit feathers around the plunging décolletage.

Pleased though she was with the bodice, it was the skirt that was her pride and joy. A belt of whisper-soft eider feathers skirted the hips, where whole families of house martins were lovingly sacrificed, their plumes smoothed carefully to ensure that the light would catch them in the most flattering and slimming way possible. From the hip the skirt suddenly flared out into the striking black and white of hoopoe and moorhen, accented with the gems of her collection – sapphire and copper feathers from a single kingfisher, secured one bright morning on a secluded river bank with a single shot from an air rifle and only a few startled ducks to bear witness. The back of the dress, a whole peacock tail fanning out and spreading across the floorboards, was breathtaking.

It was her most beautiful creation yet and, entering the room in hushed reverence, she set down the glass tray on her dressing table and circled the dress, her hand reaching out to correct the lie of a stray feather or two. The pigeon had been intended for a flash of colour on one shoulder, a spray of purple to set against the buttercup of the oriole, but now she was not so certain that the contrast would be a good one. She sat down. This would take some thinking out.

It was all the sparrow's fault. She would never have begun the project had it not carelessly lost some tail feathers for her to pick up. She had been in the park one lunchtime, sitting on her own as usual, and had spotted them lying on a bench. She had examined her finds with care, marvelling at their sheen, their delicacy. The feathers, broken and yet still breathtaking in their intricacy, had quickly become a makeshift brooch, arranged into a jaunty coil and tucked into the buttonhole that she had conveniently found in her coat lapel.

At work a few of the girls noticed it. Noticed her. Commented on how pretty it looked. She began to wonder if there was a little hope of lunch meetings, leisurely coffees, gossiping over bagels brought back from the local deli. When she got home she took the feathers out, arranged them more carefully and glued them to a brooch backing salvaged from her jewellery box. She took to wearing the sparrow brooch every day, although after the first week no one commented anymore. A few days later, wondering if something new would spark their interest, she went to the park in search of more feathers and found, instead, an injured yellowhammer. Picking it up, she realised with a start how beautiful its plumage was, from the lemon and chestnut breast to the black ticking running across its face and the striking lightning flash of a tail. She knew that here she had a gem of nature, beauty that no jeweller on earth would be able to copy.

Smiling softly, caressing the bird with one finger, she slipped it into her pocket, where it lay, trembling.

She had pinned the yellowhammer spray, accented with beads from a long-neglected choker of her grandmother's, into a beret that had hung for too long unworn in her closet. Sandra at the desk next to hers had invited her for a drink after work and asked her where she found her unusual accessories. Jane from accounts had picked the beret up off her desk and murmured something about a vintage shop that her aunt ran. She had asked whether Jennifer had considered taking orders. She had smiled.

'I only work with stray feathers,' she lied, 'I don't really think I'd be able to get enough to make for anyone else.'

'Ah, yes,' Jane had said, 'found object art. It's all the rage isn't it?'

Jennifer had nodded. They're my feathers, she had thought. I found them and they're mine.

She became more ambitious. From a moorhen, caught unawares at the local park, she had fashioned intricate cuffs for a boring black cardigan that she picked up in a charity shop. A robin, foolish enough to venture onto the feeding table she erected on her patio, provided enough red flashes to make a tiny festive wreath brooch for the Christmas party. She learned to sew and to weave, learned how to use wire work and beads with her beautiful feathers to fashion breathtaking original pieces that would draw admiring glances over morning coffee. She became increasingly cunning in her pursuit of ever-more beautiful and rare pieces. She learned to use snares and poisons. She mastered the art of mimicking bird calls. She joined a gun club. As a sideline, she learned to cook game.

Then she saw the peacock.

She had taken the day off work to visit a bird sanctuary, hoping to pick up some stray exotic feathers and, maybe, a few ideas for new creations. The place had disappointed her. Most of the birds were common enough. A few eider ducks huddled miserably by a stagnant pond, some collared doves walking freely round the place like so many clergy on a day trip. She had made up her mind to go home when she spotted the peacock. He was strutting towards her, legs kicking forward deliberately, head jerking upwards and downwards, his tail spread like a train behind him. She gasped, struck by the rich cobalt of his breast feathers, the fritillary of plumes on his head. Then he stopped, stood stock still, and, with a loud clatter of quill against quill, lifted his great flowing tail and spread it out like a Japanese fan. The eyes at the end of each feather looked into hers, a hundred golden orbs waving hypnotically back and forth.

She stared at the feathers: long and lustrous. The cobalt was shot through with emerald, shimmering in the summer sun. The frills on each quill waved like strands of silk wafted in the breeze. They were more beautiful even than her beloved kingfisher plumes. She bowed slightly to him, marvelling at how perfect he was.

She returned after dark, with bolt cutters, the gun in her bag. The theft made the national news. She tutted with her colleagues over it in the office the next day, trying not to think of the satin-feathered train that would hang from the beloved dress in her bedroom.

It was midnight before she finally made up her mind about the pigeon feathers. She had gone hunting through her haberdashery store for some Indian silk ribbons in delicate damsons and golds that she had bought at a craft fair: attracted by their brilliance and rich hues. Since she had discovered her new fascination they had lain, forgotten, in a craft drawer, but now she remembered them, and knew that their amethyst strands would be a perfect match for the violet and steel of the pigeon.

Working quickly she stitched the silks and feathers into a layered rosette and carefully attached it to the strap of the dress at the point where it was most likely to draw attention to the shoulder blade. She stepped back. It was perfect, a chocolate and cream creation accented with teal, ultramarine and buttercup yellow, the plunging neckline a perfect counterpoint to the swooping cobalt and emerald train of peacock, the hemline of moorhen breast feathers fluttering in the slight breeze through the window. She reached out a hand, hardly daring to touch it, it was so beautiful. She had intended to wear it to the office party, but now she knew it was too wondrous a creation for that. She did not wish to share it with others. She lay back on her bed, curled an arm under her neck and gazed at the dress, silhouetted in the moonlight shining through the open curtains until, finally, she fell asleep.

She woke in the middle of the night to the sound of rustling. Dew-eyed from sleep she blinked into the darkness, fearful that mice might nibble her precious gown, ready to defend it.

By the open window, the dark figure of a human form shifted slightly, turning itself towards her. She heard the rustle again, and another sound, sharper, higher in pitch.

She lifted her head from the pillows, straining to see into the night. The form quivered. It shuffled forwards, shaking more violently, the rustling rising, becoming a sharp clattering in her ears. The fan of peacock feathers rose up behind the shadow of the dress, and with a loud crack it shattered away into the room. She felt a quill gash her cheek as it passed her, embedding itself firmly into the pillow. She grasped for the light, unable to cry out.

There was a grating sound as the dress tore away from the dummy, and again she heard the high-pitched sound she had noticed before. A chirping. An insistent, bird-like screaming. The sheet of feather-fabric rose into the air, bucked and flapped, spread itself out, all but blocking the light from the window, and quivered loudly, the rattle of quill against quill deafening in the small room. Through her terror, she marvelled at how fluid it was, how beautifully it moved, how soft it would have been to wear.

It was the last thing she thought before a hundred thousand sharpened spines exploded across the room towards her.

ON THE RUN FROM THE FASHION POLICE

✂

Lorraine Jenkin

'MRS LINDA MARSHALL – REMOVE THE MOHAIR JUMPER AND PUT YOUR HANDS IN THE AIR! THIS IS THE FASHION POLICE!'

Everyone spun around, trying to see where the noise was coming from and at whom it was directed. Customers peered out of shops not knowing whether to be fearful or excited. The tannoy blazed out again across the street and Linda Marshall flinched once more.

'I repeat, remove the mohair jumper and put your hands in the air.'

Looking round, she couldn't see anyone else wearing mohair, so Linda dropped her carrier bag and nervously put her hands up. She still wasn't certain it was directed at her – surely it was a prank, but one didn't like to take risks.

'*I said, remove the mohair, lady.*' The voice driving through the loudhailer was getting cross with her now, as Linda sneaked another look round. Two women dressed in fantasy black-leather police outfits strode out from behind a large van, their stiletto heels clattering on the road, as they pointed their futuristic guns at her. A man walked up to Linda, his television camera trained on her, giving her nowhere to hide. In her confusion she took off her mohair jumper, brushing the residual fluff from her face as she returned her hands to the air. She wished that her t-shirt reached the waistband of her trousers, knowing that the camera would easily pick up the mottled excess that had been sitting there since the birth of her second child.

The two policewomen sashayed up the street towards her, cold in their fishnet stockings and low-cut jackets and the penny dropped. Ah, the *Fashion Police* – television's most recent makeover show. The ritual humiliation of people with no style, or no means to develop a style, getting poked, prodded and generally laughed at on primetime TV for the prize of a £3,000 wardrobe.

The dark-haired beauty with the pointy breastplate and the thigh-high boots walked up to Linda.

'Linda Marshall, you are being arrested by the Fashion Police for crimes against style. You stand accused of wearing comfortable clothes with no regard for your colouring, shape or other people's pleasure. What do you have to say in your defence?'

Linda squirmed. It was like being back at school. She picked up her jumper and wriggled back into it. The Fashion Police's disdain was less embarrassing than her short t-shirt.

'I, well, I was cold this morning. My, er, jeans were on the line and, well, I was in a rush.'

The blonde cackled through the tannoy and walked up to her.

'Linda, even Eskimos don't wear mohair anymore, especially with a kitten on the front. Sorry, not good enough I'm afraid.' She removed some pink-feathered handcuffs from her belt and brandished them for the camera. 'Linda Marshall, are you happy to be arrested by the Fashion Police?' At this point, the feisty duo pointed their guns at her, then at the sky, then blew a seductive breath over the top of them and winked at each other, just as they had with every other victim on their Tuesday night show.

Linda took a deep breath and considered the options. This was real now. National humiliation for the price of £3,000 worth of clothes. Everyone would be laughing at her back-fat and hairy legs for the prize of £3,000 worth of clothes. Was knowing how bad you really looked from behind worth £3,000 of clothes? Possibly. Probably.

'Okay,' she answered slowly, still not *really* sure that it was the right thing to do. 'Yes, I'm ready to be arrested by the Fashion Police.'

'Aaaand, CUT,' shouted a man with a clipboard. 'Okay, ladies, thank you. That was good. Cindy, Bella, you were great – very slick. Right, let's get back in the van, it's bloody cold.'

Linda felt forgotten as Bella and Cindy were wrapped in coats to keep out the same wind that whipped through her kitten jumper. 'Could I put my hat on now, please?' she asked meekly, rummaging in her bag.

'Hold on,' Bella said, 'should we do it again with that hat on? It's a beauty! I've not seen one of those for, ooh, fifteen years.'

'No, we need to keep her element of surprise in. Pity though, it is awful isn't it – perhaps we can incorporate it into a later take?' replied the man with the clipboard as he walked off.

Cindy stared at Linda. 'Perhaps just unroll the edges a bit though? Make it less of a City supporters' club hat, eh?' she said, not able to stop herself fiddling. 'And do you have a jacket to put over that jumper? Maybe a trench coat – with a belt?' Linda cringed: perhaps she should have refused after all – this wasn't going to be the easy money that she had first thought.

Linda was plonked on a couch in a plush studio full of cushions and drapes – but she felt far from comfortable. They had asked her to keep the mohair jumper on but the heat from the lights was making it itch. Cindy and Bella were being plucked and tugged into shape by a gaggle of stylish women wearing black. Good lord, thought Linda, if this is what it takes to look as good as they do, forget it. I'd never get out of the door. A woman wandered over to her and, without introducing herself, rubbed a brush over her face releasing a cloud of powder. Linda coughed and earned herself a roll of disdain from the woman's eyes.

A large screen was pushed in front of the sofa and a number of shouts indicated that filming was about to restart.

Linda sat on her hands feeling very small amongst the cushions and then there was a clack clack as Bella and Cindy walked over to her, perfectly groomed and manicured. They bent to embrace Linda as if they were longstanding friends instead of jailors.

'Now, Linda, how are you feeling? Are you up for the makeover, or are you a little nervous?' Linda's reply was lost as she mumbled amongst their next statement.

'Now, you are probably wondering who set you up for this?' Linda nodded. 'Well, they have been filming you for a while, so let's check this out!'

The screen in front of her lit up and showed a scene at a barbeque. It was in Linda's garden and she was walking out of the house carrying a platter of kebabs on skewers. Her friends, Sandy and Ella, were sitting around a table giggling into their glasses of wine and winking at the camera. The shot then panned back to Linda and she could hear Lucy's voice talking quietly into the video camera.

And, this is Linda, wearing her best tight vest. A Sunday market special I think. See the way it drags across the bust and stomach, yet flaps around the shoulders. See also how the bright yellow colour makes her face look the colour of wallpaper paste.

Bella patted Linda's arm.

'Do you remember that day?'

'I do. I remember her filming us too – she said that she was practising for her son's school play. I didn't realise that she was saying those things for—'

Linda had turned to put the kebabs onto the barbeque. *'See also how her shorts are nestling so snugly into her backside…and sandals with socks, well our Linda does like to be comfortable.'*

Linda didn't feel comfortable now, and she knew that there was worse to come – she'd still got that hideous sports bra on, the one she used to wear when she played squash – when her bust was two cup sizes smaller. They were going to love it when that was revealed—

Somehow she got through the ridicule that was supposed to

be the helpful bit – telling her where she went so wrong and how she could hide that roll of stomach fat without resorting to surgery, how she could make her legs, (which were now being described as dumpy), look longer. She was whisked away, feeling a little dejected, to a plush hotel for the night and was given time to sit and consider the sorry state of her fashion faux pas.

The next day Linda was released into the shops. She had a list of clothes to aim for and another of things to avoid. She was getting used to being followed by a man with a camera, and was beginning to play to it. She was told to hold things up to the light so that the camera could see what she was looking at and then hold them against herself before putting things back on the rail. She knew that this allowed Cindy and Bella to mock her choices and groan at the thought that she might still think that horizontal stripes suited her.

By lunchtime, however, Linda was buying style classics with the ease of a professional shopper. 'She's really taken on board what we said,' confided Bella to Cindy, as they watched Linda from behind a clothes rail, 'I've never seen such a confident transformation!'

'Yes,' replied Bella, flicking her tonged hair away from her face, 'it's as if this caterpillar were completely ready to emerge from her chrysalis. I'd like to see her accessorising a little more confidently, though.' Cindy nodded, then they spun their guns at each other in delight as Linda held a chunky gold necklace against a blue blouse. 'Do you know, I think this criminal might get away with just a community sentence!'

Linda returned to the studio with bags full of clothes and a big smile on her face—

*

It was a Tuesday night when Linda walked into her lounge carrying a tray of champagne flutes. She handed them out to her friends, taking care not to spill any on her cashmere dress.

'Thank you,' said Ella, wiping the mascara from under her eye with a wetted tissue. 'That was FANTASTIC! I haven't laughed so much since Sandy had that guy from the DIY team fall through her ceiling!'

'No, me neither! But Linda – that sports bra! Where on earth did you get it? It was hideous!' laughed Lucy.

'Hmm, I'm afraid I found that one in the bottom of my wardrobe – damn thing itched all day! Not sure it was worth three grand to be seen on national television with a badly fitting grey sports bra on...and anyway, Lucy – did you *have* to be quite so rude in that video we made? Laughing at my bingo wings and saddlebags in that jumpsuit in the dinner party scene – *they* are real I'll have you know! I didn't put *them* on for the camera!'

Lucy giggled, taking a large sip of the champagne. 'Well, at least you didn't have to pretend you had returned to being a call girl when your husband stopped wanting sex! My challenge was definitely the worst – at least you got £3,000 worth of clothes. I only got a measly £700 for my story.'

'True – but I think Sandy definitely drew the longest straw – she got a new kitchen! I think for this year's challenge we'll have to give Lucy the first choice of what she does! So come on ladies, what's it to be? We've all taken our employers to industrial tribunals, we've all created a village scandal, and we've now done a reality show or magazine each. What's next?

I'm still up for getting someone to sponsor some kind of non-existent plastic surgery – what do you think?'

'No, too messy,' answered Ella. 'Blackmail?'

'No – because then we're back to the "Getting Arrested" challenge, and I'm not sure I'm up for that.'

'My favourite is still the one that Sandy thought of.' The women all looked at Ella and started to giggle.

'Shall we? Can we?' asked Linda, looking around at the friends she'd known since school. They all looked at each other and nodded their approval.

'Everyone agreed then? Okay – the next challenge is to form a singing quartet and try out for a television talent show, the plan being that during filming, we each do something so awful that we get ourselves shown on the programme. Winner is the one that gets the most coverage.'

The four women stood and raised their glasses to the plan. 'To national stardom,' proposed Linda with a smile.

'To national stardom,' they repeated as their glasses chinked together, each already thinking about how to make the spotlight their own...

REUNION

✂

Rebecca Lees

Friday loomed and still Caitlin had nothing to wear. Her wardrobe had been stripped almost bare; blouses mounting to a teetering pile on the bed and dresses dangling precariously off hangers clipped over doors and curtain rails. But the swarms of cotton, silk and wool all added up to those dreaded words. Nothing To Wear.

At the scrape of a key in the front door, Caitlin's head swivelled towards her bedside alarm clock; 8.34, announced the bright green numbers. God, how was it that time already? Seemed like she'd only put the twins to bed ten minutes ago. Damn, thought Caitlin as the familiar footsteps bounded upstairs. She hadn't even put the oven on and Alex would be starving after his meeting.

'Hiya, love.' Alex's head bobbed around the door. 'Oh my God, what happened in here?' Caitlin smiled thinly as Alex plonked himself down on the edge of the bed, carelessly pulling her new Coast wrap from under his bum. 'Just trying to find something for Friday,' she explained, a little defensively. To his credit, five years of marriage had made Alex far too wise to reason that, surely, she must have something among the garments taking up four fifths of their wardrobe, or to point to her wobbly stack of once-worn shoes. Unfortunately he wasn't too wise to wonder why she was going on Friday at all.

'I knew you didn't want me to, I just knew!' Caitlin snapped, pointing accusingly at him with a grey patent heel.

Alex blew out the weary sigh of a soon-to-be-defeated man. 'It isn't that I don't want you to go,' he explained patiently. 'It's that I don't think *you* want to go, so I don't know why you're putting yourself through it.'

Caitlin busied herself straightening the arms of her navy jacket to avoid Alex's calm gaze. 'You know I have to,' she said. 'Everyone's going.' *Everyone*, she thought, scooping up a tangle of jumpers while Alex rubbed his eyes blearily. Everyone from sixth form. How long ago was it – ten years? God no, eleven. Eleven years and a little more baby weight around her middle than she'd hoped. She had shifted most of it, mainly by pushing the double buggy around the village on sanity-saving walks when maternity leave with two fractious babies became too much. But those last five pounds had waged a stubborn battle and everyone knew it got even harder in your 30s – which Caitlin was fast approaching. She grimaced at the thought of half sympathetic, half triumphant looks being cast in her direction on Friday. *Ooo, Caitlin Price has let herself go,* the glances would say. She had to look the part, she just had to.

'Right,' said Alex flatly. 'I'll go and see what's for tea, shall I?' And he rose abruptly, sending a silk scarf slithering to the floor. The door sighed to a close behind him and Caitlin was left alone amongst the rubble. Defiantly scooping her spangly River Island smock dress from the back of the wardrobe door, she bobbed her head between the hanger and the straps. It camouflaged the wobbly bit around her middle whilst showing off her trim legs to perfection. Still, it was hardly suitable for Friday and time was running out. 'Time to call in the cavalry,' Caitlin announced to no one in particular.

Delving to the bottom of her leather handbag – the luxurious one Alex had surprised her with on his return from that Italian conference last year – Caitlin scooped out her phone to text Heidi. *Help! Emerg shop 2mo lunchtime,* she thumbed, knowing the magic word would reel her friend in. Thirty seconds later she was rewarded with the reliable plink of incoming news. *I'm in! C u in D'hams at 1* ran Heidi's reply. Well that's one less thing to worry about, thought Caitlin, buttoning a crisp white shirt back onto its hanger. Then with a rush her eyes filled with tears and she plopped backwards onto the bed, narrowly avoiding the cashmere cardigan Alex's mum had given her last Christmas. It's just tiredness, she told herself, what with the dash from work to pick up Mali and Owen, then the slog of baths and bedtime stories. She gazed wistfully at the duvet, visible again following the re-imprisonment of her clothes in the wardrobe, then swiped at her eyes and followed Alex downstairs.

It was nearly ten past one by the time Caitlin zipped into Debenhams the next day, thanks to a demanding client she couldn't get off the phone. But across the Clinique counter she could see Heidi was there already, being swathed in perfume by an adoring assistant. For a few seconds Caitlin forgot to rush, basking at a distance in the charm Heidi could turn on when it suited her, even though Caitlin had seen the routine hundreds of times before. Then Heidi caught sight of her friend and the poor young man was left spraying scent into thin air, immediately forgotten.

'C'mon!' said Heidi, dashing over and linking her arm through Caitlin's. 'Haven't got long so let's head straight for Betty Jackson. I saw some gorgeous dresses there last week.'

They glided through the store, Heidi skilfully sliding garments off rails and halting every couple of minutes to inspect possible purchases draped over mannequins. Ensconced in the fitting room, Heidi settled on a stool and started firing questions at Caitlin over the curtain.

'So this Anya just phoned you up out of the blue?' she checked, drawing some Nicorette gum out of her bag.

'Yep. On Sunday,' replied Caitlin. 'Funny thing was, I knew it was her voice straight away, even after all this time.'

'Yeah well, I guess you would if she pinched the love of your life,' retorted Heidi.

Caitlin flicked back the curtain to reveal a svelte blue dress, at which Heidi nodded approvingly. '*Alex* is the love of my life,' she corrected with mock severity. 'Stefan was...er...the one that got away.'

'Mmm, if you say so,' said Heidi. 'Tell you what, my silver heels would look fab with that. You can borrow them if you like. So what did you say to her?'

'I just asked if she really wanted me there,' said Caitlin. Somehow she had been sure Anya was nodding into the phone as she confirmed, flicking that glorious red hair of hers up and down. 'She said it would be unthinkable without me. For Stef.'

She swooshed the curtain back into place and peeled off the dress ready for outfit number two.

Outside the cubicle, Heidi's phone burst into the theme tune from 'Dallas'. 'Hiya, I'm in Debenhams a minute,' Caitlin heard her say. 'With Cait. Yup. Yup. Ooo, *never.*'

With Heidi's attention diverted, there was nothing to stop Caitlin brooding about Anya's call. She could see herself now, chirping her hello into the phone then dropping onto the bottom stair in shock at the voice on the other end. It had been unmistakeable, yes, but also altered; softer now, without its teenage arrogance. A shoebox-worth of memories, carefully filed and tucked into a dark corner of the attic, had rushed uninvited into Caitlin's head as she pressed the red button to end the call. There she was, crammed with Stefan into the passport photo booth in Woolies, giggling in their school uniform grey. And there at the top of Pen y Fan, smiles tucked into their scarves to keep out the biting February wind. Even now Caitlin could picture the looping handwriting and scrawled kisses bearing witness to bygone Valentine'ses and Christmases. But when Anya had arrived, sweeping down from the posh new estate into the common room, that was that. She could have had her pick, so it was little wonder to wide-eyed classmates that she had set her sights on the most popular boy in the school, coolly overlooking the fact he already had a girlfriend.

The snap of Heidi's phone closing brought Caitlin back to the changing room and she revealed a skirt suit to Heidi, waiting for the expert opinion. Heidi pulled a face.

'Oh, God no,' she said. 'That jacket does nothing for you, Cait. That was Claire; you'll never *guess* what Phil's done this time.'

But Caitlin's vacant 'Hmm?' suggested it was a tale best kept for their next girls' night out, and Heidi reluctantly turned from her gossip back to Caitlin's old boyfriend.

'So that was that, then?' she asked. 'You just ran off to uni and never saw him again?'

'Pretty much.' Out of the unflattering suit, Caitlin zipped herself back into her trousers. 'I thought it was the best revenge at the time. Thought he'd realise what a huge mistake he'd made, while I was off having the time of my life.' She sighed. 'Didn't think for a minute they'd live happily ever after.'

Caitlin slung the blue dress over her arm and handed the unwanted suit to a hovering assistant. Abruptly, she turned to Heidi and hugged her. 'Thanks, Heid,' she said.

'What, for shopping?' Heidi teased.

'You know what I mean,' Caitlin replied. 'Alex...he doesn't get the way...it's not really about the clothes, is it?' Her words came out in a rush. 'He thinks I can be so vacuous sometimes, fussing over which bag goes with what, and dithering over my heels, and especially for wanting something new for this damn thing. He doesn't get that it's all a...a—'

'...mask?' suggested Heidi. 'Just one big cover up?' She sighed in sympathy. 'No. But he's a *man*, Cait. He thinks worrying about what to wear means debating whether to tuck his shirt in or not.' She squeezed Caitlin's hand then broke into a wry grin. 'Heck, this is *far* too deep for this time of day – and without a bottle of red!' she said. 'C'mon, you pay for the dress and I'll shout you a sarnie from O'Briens. I'm starving.'

On Friday Caitlin awoke before the alarm, foggily clawing her way to the surface of sleep. Something had disturbed her dream, but by the time the familiar outlines of her bedroom emerged it was already gone. Usually she would snuggle back under the covers, delighting in the cosy quiet before Alex and the twins pitched into her day, but such a treat had no allure today and she was up, tiptoeing downstairs in search of distraction. She pushed open the kitchen door and was confronted with a fierce orange September sunrise. Why had she never noticed before that the sun did this, invading its way through the patio doors and burning the walls? After all, she was often up at this time, packing the twins' spare clothes for nursery or rummaging through the ironing pile for a clean shirt for work. She realised she had been sleepwalking: first through the exhausting chaos of the twins' first year and now through the job that had once impassioned her but had lately started to leave her slightly dazed.

Sliding open the patio door, Caitlin settled on the doorstep, a forgotten cup of tea soon turning stone cold beside her. From her perch at the top of the sloping garden she could see over the fence and away down the valley, her gaze skimming dotted streets and trees until it reached the tiny speck of the A470. Caitlin hadn't even wanted to move here; it had seemed too far both from work in one direction and from the emergency comfort of her parents in the other. But Alex had gently persisted and now – today, of all days – Caitlin realised he had been right. A dormant sense of home started to stir. And with it crept up a sense of self – the old self who would never, ever, have failed to notice the sunrise.

Alex's tap on the shoulder, although gentle, startled her back to the importance of the day. 'What are you doing out here, love?' he asked. 'It's a bit chilly, isn't it?' For a second Caitlin was on the brink of describing the sunrise, now dimmed to the faded blue start of the new day. Then she clocked a blob of last night's toothpaste, suspended down the front of Alex's pyjama top, and the intimacy snapped. 'Just thinking,' she smiled. 'I'd best go and get ready, I guess. Gosh, yes, it's later than I thought.'

'Well I'll make you a fresh cuppa and bring it up,' said Alex.

'Thanks, love,' replied Caitlin and drifted through the kitchen towards the hall, smiling a good morning at Mali and Owen as they heaved cereal packets out of the bottom cupboard. At the top of the stairs she realised she hadn't told Alex to put fresh pull-ups in Owen's bag. She was about to shout down when she was struck by a new possibility. *Maybe he'll check for himself,* she thought, and closed the bathroom door.

Just before eleven, after covering a long stretch of the M4, Caitlin pulled up in old, familiar territory. She could still feel the reassuring hug Alex had given her at the front door which, to her surprise, hadn't been accompanied by a last-minute bid to change her mind. Beeping the car locked Caitlin smoothed down the front of her black dress; more a futile bid to quell the knot in her stomach than to iron away imaginary crinkles. Her only nod to colour was the bold red stitching on black heels, the pair that reminded her she'd been a flirty young woman before morphing into a dribble-spattered mum. She had planned a more vibrant outfit, suspecting many of her old friends would arrive in a blast of colour. But when it came to putting on the blue dress, it had felt too unnatural; too forced, and even Heidi would have had to concede that Caitlin's trusted knee-length A-line was the best option.

With a deep breath Caitlin plunged into the line gently winding its way towards St Peter's. She passed into the welcoming cool of the porch, tuning in to the quiet hymn of muffled sobs within. Stalling her own tears by concentrating on the notorious heel-trapping grates that lined the aisle, Caitlin processed nearer to the waiting coffin and settled into a pew.

THE RED HAT

✂

Barbara McGaughey

As soon as she stepped out of her front door Miss Phillips knew that the Rolls Royce was there again. The air of the street was charged; there was a buzz of anticipation behind the closed doors and the twitching curtains. She climbed sedately into her small blue Ford and prepared to set off for her weekly shopping trip to the town. In the driving mirror she saw its silver shimmer parked at the kerb six doors away, and marvelled that the neighbours still got so churned up at the thought that Edward Penvelyn was visiting his mother. He'd been the pride and joy of their corner of Carmarthenshire now for nearly twenty years, and Miss Phillips, like everybody else, had watched with interest his progress from chapel concert, via drama school and soap opera, to Hollywood stardom. Everybody knew that he was good to his mother, flying her out to California every year for a holiday and visiting her each time he was in Britain.

'He've been good to me, Louie, specially since his dad died.' Dilys Jones (for Jones was Edward's real surname) told her.

'I did wonder 'ow it would be when he married Angela, but she's a nice girl under all that make-up and she makes me very welcome in Bel Air. But it's too 'ot for me out there. I'm always glad to come 'ome.'

Miss Phillips and Mrs Jones had known each other all their lives, growing up in the pebble-dashed semis where they still lived. They had both gone away for a while, Louise to college and Dilys when she became Mrs Jones. Both had come back to look after ageing parents and in time inherited their semis, but whereas Dilys shared hers with three children and a jolly husband, Louise stayed single and gave piano lessons for a living. Small Eddie Jones had been one of her pupils, a cheery vivid little boy, though not very musical, and she was sincerely pleased at his success.

The Rolls was still there when Miss Phillips drove home at noon and the street was full of people, mostly women, standing in groups and staring at the Jones house with as much excitement as if it were on fire. A small child wandered into the road, causing Miss Phillips to swerve. She tooted at the inattentive mother and drew up outside her house. As she transferred her parcels from the car she bumped into her next-door neighbour, who was carrying such a big pile of clothes that she couldn't see where she was going.

'Sorry,' said the woman breathlessly. 'There's the most marvellous clothes in there. Must be worth thousands!' and she was off with her trophies to get them home before her luck changed.

Miss Phillips had two little pupils that afternoon, both so excited that the film star had come home that they could barely see the piano keys. The patient Miss Phillips did her best, but she was aware all the time of people moving up and down the street, of laughter and excited voices. She wondered if Eddie's wife had come with him this time. If so the neighbours had two film stars for the price of one – for the glamorous Angela Thorne was a star in her own right, even more famous than Edward.

By teatime the street was quiet, and when Miss Phillips looked out of the front door again, the Rolls Royce had gone. No sooner had she closed the door, however, than there was a loud knock and Dilys Jones bounced in beaming.

'Saw you at the door, Louie. I been looking out for you all afternoon.'

Miss Phillips surveyed her fat, flustered friend. 'Sit down, Dil,' she said, 'and tell me all about it. I saw the car and all the people waiting to see Eddie.'

'More fool them,' said Eddie's mother. ''Twasn't 'im or Angela this time, but only the chauffeur with this 'uge wicker basket in the boot. It was so 'eavy the poor bloke almost gave 'imself a hernia carrying it into the house. Anyway, it was crammed full of clothes belonging to Angela, clothes she didn't need any more, almost brand new, most of them, with designer labels 'an all. Trouble was they was too small to fit me or either of the girls, and Angela had said I could do what I liked with them, so I asked a couple of people in and it's been like Oxfam over there all day. I saw this lovely tailored grey trouser suit early on and I could see how good it would look on you – now shut up, Louie, don't go telling me you never wear trousers – so I put it away upstairs, and you can come now and try it on.'

She paused, breathless, then, as Miss Phillips opened her

mouth to refuse, she added. 'Come anyway and see this lovely big shawl I've kept for myself. All the colours of the rainbow it is.'

Miss Phillips took the line of least resistance; she could argue when she got there.

The Jones house was quiet but the sitting room was unusually dishevelled, with bits of discarded women's clothing abandoned all over the furniture. Mrs Jones swept these together into a heap on the floor. 'Charity shop,' she said. She shoved Miss Phillips into a chair and gave her a one-garment fashion display of her shawl. It was a beautiful, expensive thing of mauves and greens and blues, with a long, silken fringe. Miss Phillips showed her sincere admiration and her exuberant friend shoved it into her hands 'for a feel' while she rushed upstairs to get the trouser suit.

Left alone Miss Phillips gathered herself together for the tussle of wills to come. She draped the shawl carefully over the back of the chair and saw, out of the corner of her eye, something red sitting on a vase on the mantelpiece. She got up for a better look and found the most beautiful hat she had ever seen. It was made of red straw and red ribbon and that was all, a wisp of a thing, wicked and provocative. It spoke to Miss Phillips of forbidden love and secrets, of Paris, where she had never been and of lovers she had never known. Inside was a little label, 'Property of Metro Goldwyn Meyer' it announced. When Mrs Jones came in with the trouser suit there was no argument; to Miss Phillips it had become an irrelevance.

'Dilys,' she said, 'I want this hat.'

Ten minutes later she left, carrying it in a brown paper bag.

From the doorstep behind her came a wail. 'You're mad, Louie, and where are you going to wear it?'

As soon as she tried the hat on at home she knew she must change her hairstyle. Her hair was too long, too lank and too boring for it. On her head the hat looked like what her mother would have described as 'a cockle on a rock'. There was nobody in the village or indeed in the nearby market town to whom she could entrust her newly precious hair. She made herself a cup of Ovaltine and consulted the *Yellow Pages*. In the city thirty miles away she found a name that sounded promising. 'Mario di Antonio Nocero, hair stylist of excellence,' she read.

The next day was Saturday and she had no pupils to consider. She phoned the salon early and, after a long and tenacious exchange with the receptionist, made an appointment to have her hair styled by Signor Mario himself. She drove into town with the hat on the seat beside her. She rolled down the car window to let the breeze cool her hot cheeks. She felt truly alive for the first time in years.

To her relief Signor Mario turned out to be charming, a brisk continental who was delighted to create a hairstyle to suit a hat. Propelling himself around her on a little stool with wheels, he snipped and combed and brushed and dried and sprayed. When he finally stood back and handed her the mirror to see herself at every angle, she saw an elegant, long-necked woman with a swirl of smooth hair framing her face.

'Now,' said Signor Mario, reverently placing the hat on the brown hair. He beamed at her in the mirror, pleased himself at the transformation. 'You look beautiful, Madame,' he said. And indeed she did. She smiled back at him.

'Thank you,' she said.

She felt slightly less grateful when she saw the bill but she hastily fished out her credit card, put the hat back in the bag and stepped into the street in search of refreshment. She found that she could not resist looking at herself in every shop window she passed and each time she felt a rush of delight at her reflection. In Marks and Spencers' café she indulged herself with café latte and carrot cake and considered her next move. If she was to present herself and her red hat in public it had to be soon, while the fine weather held – red straw and ribbons would not survive wind and rain. Something else occurred to her. Her best brown herringbone would look ludicrous with the hat so she needed new clothes and she couldn't really afford anything that would live up to it. Deflated, she rode down the escalator and saw the SALE signs on the next floor. At once she found a straight, figure-hugging little black dress, much reduced. She forced herself to go through the embarrassment of trying it on and was dismayed to see it hang limply and shapelessly on her. She was disheartened enough to call the sales assistant to have a look.

'It's your bra, Madam,' said the girl at once. 'You need a wired one with uplift.'

When Miss Phillips got back into her car she had three bags: one for the hat, one for the black dress and one for a confection of wire, black lace and elastic such as she had never owned before. Driving home she said to herself, 'Talk about all dressed up and nowhere to go!'

And then, in a flash, it came to her. She knew where and when she would appear in all her finery.

The Reverend Ifor ap Llewelyn paced nervously up and down

the deacons' room. It was 10.27 on Sunday morning and the service was due to start at 10.30. His two surviving deacons, both a bit doddery, looked anxiously to him for leadership. But the Reverend had never been a leader; he was gentle, scholarly and, at the moment, anxious.

'There's nearly fifty of them out there this morning. That's more than we've had since the carol service,' said one deacon.

'Perhaps she've been taken ill suddenly,' suggested the other.

The connecting door to the chapel was opened violently and the minister's wife appeared, all heaving bosom and uncompromising hat.

'What's the matter, Ifor?' she demanded. 'Are you ill? You've got dozens out there for once, thanks to this nice weather, and if you don't look sharp they'll all go home again – and think what that will do to the collection!'

The Reverend Ifor looked ashamed of her, but old habits die hard.

'It's Miss Phillips,' he said. 'She's not here to play the organ. She's always here when I arrive and she starts the pre-service music at 10:20 sharp once she's given me the list of hymns to announce. Didn't you realise there was no music as you came in?'

His wife shrugged. 'Not particularly,' she said. 'She's such a little mouse and she plays such boring music.' She returned to the attack. 'Go in there at once and start the service and I'll send somebody round to her house to see what's happened. Well, don't just stand there. Move!' and she went back into the chapel, banging the door behind her. The minister looked after her with real dislike. How, he wondered, could the pretty girl he had met at college thirty years ago have turned into that? He picked up his New Testament and prepared to follow. The side door opened quickly and a smart, slim, youngish woman in a red hat came in. It wasn't until she began to speak that the three men recognised Miss Phillips. She was flustered and apologetic.

'Oh, Mr ap Llewelyn, I'm so sorry I'm late,' she said. 'I was ready twenty minutes ago but I couldn't find my car keys. Do you know, I'd left them in the ignition all night and that was the last place I thought of looking. Wasn't I lucky that they were still there? I can't think what came over me! I've never done such a thing before in my life!' They stared at her. They had never heard Miss Phillips speak for so long in one go.

'Anyway,' she said smiling, 'better late than never. Here's the list of hymns. I'll go in first, shall I?'

The appearance of a fashionably-dressed stranger on the organ bench caused a ripple of interest, but chapel congregations have been well brought up, and once the service began they confined themselves to the occasional raised eyebrow and answering shrug. Two women, however, continued to study the side view of the slim woman in the red hat. Dilys Jones, in her family pew, rehearsed the story she would have to tell Eddie on their transatlantic phone call that evening. The minister's wife, from her front seat, could see who the organist was and could also see the covert glances her husband gave towards the jaunty hat.

At the end of the service the congregation stayed much longer than usual. Many remained in their seats, waiting to verify the claim that the red-hatted figure was Miss Phillips the Music. In her organ mirror Louise Phillips could see them all hanging about and she wondered what piece of sacred music would suitably close the proceedings. After a brief hesitation she began to play softly and with great feeling *'Somewhere over the Rainbow'*.

FLICKER

✂

Jo Lloyd

'With those fat legs,' said Gwenda.

'Hush,' said Ruth, glancing over at the waitress her mother was talking about, a teenager with blackened hair and quite normal legs.

Recently Gwenda had taken to saying the word 'fat' as if she'd bitten on a piece of grit. The cancer had started in her breast. Now it was in her bones. Suddenly everyone looked fat to her. 'She's too fat to be an actress,' she would say, watching television. 'She's an MP,' Ruth would say. 'Then she's too fat to be an MP,' Gwenda would reply. Or, passing someone unwrapping a sandwich in the street, 'Eating! That's what made her so fat.'

Every time she said it, Ruth, who had been slim for two decades, practised Pilates, drank only Evian or dry champagne, felt as if her mother was prodding at her ribs.

Gwenda had lost weight again since Ruth had last seen her. The candles in the café threw deep shadows on her face. Her legs, under her trousers, were old woman legs, bird legs. Ruth didn't like to look at them.

They were in town to buy her an outfit for a christening. She had rung Ruth up, saying, 'I don't know what to wear. Why did they invite me? I've got nothing to wear.'

'Of course you do,' said Ruth, thinking of the big wardrobe in her mother's bedroom, its doors held open by the clothes pressing out of it, clothes Gwenda wore all the time, clothes she didn't wear any more, clothes she had thought she might wear one day.

'I want to look nice,' said Gwenda. 'It'll probably be the last time people see me.'

Ruth leaned back on the sofa, looking at the opposite wall. 'What about your green suit?'

'That won't do. Not in that awful draughty church.' Gwenda felt the cold now, had no resources to spare for it. 'I don't know why they have to have it there.'

'You could wear a coat with it,' said Ruth.

'I don't want to wear a coat. I want to look smart.'

'Your good coat,' said Ruth, noticing a dark patch high on the wall, 'the one you wore to Dad's funeral.' The gutter must be leaking, she thought.

'You can't wear a black coat to a christening.'

'You think they'll have a coat inspector on the door? You can wear what you like. You of all people.'

'You don't know anything,' said Gwenda.

Or perhaps, thought Ruth, it was the rain, blowing in from the west, getting in under the paint. When Ben came over she'd have him go up and take a look at it. That wasn't, she thought, inappropriate.

'Anyway, all my clothes are too big now.'

'So buy something new,' said Ruth. Or perhaps she should just call the roofer. No ambiguity there.

'How can I go shopping?' said Gwenda. 'All on my own.'

'Jackie would take you. Or Delyth.'

'I couldn't get anything here. I'd have to go into Cardiff. All on my own.'

'Or with Jackie,' Ruth said. 'Or Delyth.'

'Anyway, there's nothing in Cardiff. It's not like it used to be. You don't know.'

Ruth's brother brought Gwenda up in the car. It was a two-hour drive, even straight along the motorway, even with Aled racing down the fast lane with eyes fixed, flashing his lights at anything that got in his way. They arrived after dark, barely speaking. Aled said he couldn't stay, Caroline would be waiting, he had an early meeting. He brought Gwenda's bag in and then left.

'That was a terrible journey,' said Gwenda. 'The way Aled drives. Really. I don't feel safe.'

'How about a cup of tea,' said Ruth. 'I've lit a fire in the conservatory.'

'I'm not doing that journey again,' said Gwenda.

Ruth would be taking her back next week. 'Perhaps my car will be more comfortable,' she said.

'I don't see why it would be,' said Gwenda. 'At least Aled's car is fast.'

The first shop was a place Ruth didn't usually go. She had thought, for some reason, that the bright stiff clothes, propped in colour groups like paint cards, might appeal to her mother.

An assistant in nurse's shoes approached, spoke to Gwenda in a loud voice that fell, at the end, to a pat. Ruth felt her mother take breath. 'We're fine for now,' said Ruth quickly, smiling. She steered Gwenda away, around the shop, pointing out this and that. Gwenda sniffed. 'Old woman clothes,' she said. She was right, Ruth thought. They were uniforms to cover the wounded.

The second shop seemed to have undergone a sulky transformation since Ruth had last been in. Salesgirls drifted in the shadows, watching the door, their eyes sooty with discontent. The clothes, folded on tables, seemed to be missing parts, sleeves, backs, hems. Gwenda picked up a woollen dress, torn like a spiderweb, and held it out towards Ruth. 'Have you ever seen a person this shape?'

'Okay,' said Ruth, holding up her hands. 'Let's go somewhere else.'

'Not till I've had a sit down,' said her mother. 'You seem to forget I'm ill.'

The café was warm, golden from the candles flickering on the walls, and busy. In a mirror behind Gwenda, Ruth was startled, for a second, to spot among the shoppers a familiar, unwelcome face. Not the face she prepared so carefully at home, but the one that came out when she wasn't looking, the tired eyes, the drawn mouth. She looked away, feeling the face put on some treacherous expression of its own. Ben had told her he'd been afraid to approach her at first, the way she scowled. Perhaps she could get something done about that.

She picked up the menu. 'You'll like it here,' she said. 'You can get a proper tea. Scones. Crumpets.'

'Crumpets?' said Gwenda. 'I can't eat crumpets.'

'Well they're not compulsory. How about a scone?'

'I just want tea.'

'I'll order some toast.' Her mother had had no breakfast, half a bowl of soup for lunch. 'And a piece of cake. We can share.'

'I won't want it.'

Ruth rarely ate cake herself. Sometimes when she was out with Ben. She didn't need him to see the effort it took to keep looking this way. He cheerfully ate cake and biscuits, chocolate, sweets, crisps. He would sprawl in jeans and a t-shirt, perfectly comfortable in the world, while she, increasingly, arranged herself on the surface of it.

No one had said it aloud yet – Your nephew? Your son? – but she saw the question quiver on their faces.

When the tea came Gwenda complained. 'This isn't skimmed milk,' she said.

'Why do you want skimmed milk?' asked Ruth.

'I always drink skimmed.'

'Mother,' said Ruth. 'You're the last person who should be drinking skimmed milk.'

'Just tell that fat girl to bring some.'

The milk arrived in a tiny jug. Ruth watched the girl walk away. She thought perhaps her mother had been right about the skirt.

They drank their tea. All around was a soft murmuring and clinking. People comparing reports, discussing strategy. They dipped their heads together, waved their hands, making shadow puppets on the walls.

'There's a nice shop near here we can try,' said Ruth.

'I don't know why we don't just go to Marks,' said Gwenda.

'You could do that at home,' said Ruth. She wanted to take her mother somewhere special, the kind of place Gwenda would have been intimidated by, would have dismissed as snobby.

'Not that they're what they used to be,' said Gwenda.

And perhaps, too, she wanted to show her mother where she had got to, what she had achieved, how money could split the world open like a log.

When Ruth was applying to universities, Gwenda took her shopping for interview clothes. Ruth hadn't given it a thought. Every day she wore the same thing, jeans, a man's shirt and waistcoat from Oxfam. Her friends all wore something very similar. Gwenda told her she couldn't possibly go to an interview like that. She would need a new skirt and top, shoes, a coat. Her usual clothes would not do out in the world, the outside world, England.

They went to Cardiff. Gwenda picked out the clothes they might be able to afford and Ruth trudged in and out of cubicles to display them. 'For goodness sake stand up straight,' Gwenda kept saying. And then she would frown. It was as if she was surprised each time, with each new ill-fitting skirt and blouse, at the sight of Ruth, lumpen, fidgeting, tied up like a parcel. She would move behind her daughter, tweak at a hem, a sleeve. 'Perhaps a different size,' she would say, in a puzzled voice. She seemed to have been imagining someone else all these years.

With each new outfit, Ruth felt herself prickle and swell, as if the clothes raised an allergic reaction. By the end of the morning she was two sizes bigger, hunched, miserable. They had bought nothing.

They went to a cavernous dark restaurant under Queen

Street, took their place in a line of women with carrier bags and packages, dazed, singed faces.

'Have whatever you want,' Gwenda said. 'We may as well treat ourselves.'

Ruth chose a salad. Her mother looked at it. 'Are you sure that's all? No chips or anything?' They sat at their table in silence, staring through the gloom at the other shoppers, preparing to go out into it again, to get through it.

As the day went on, Gwenda seemed increasingly defeated by the clothes, the prices, the shop assistants, Ruth's intransigence. She began to lose her clear idea of what they were doing. 'I don't know,' she said. 'Perhaps some smart trousers would be better.' She turned the price tickets over and sighed. It became a negotiation. If Ruth had the dearer top, then she'd have to have the cheaper coat. 'Will you please stop slouching,' Gwenda said.

After the interviews, Ruth never wore those clothes again. They were scratchy, rigid, hostile. She kept packing and unpacking them as she moved from place to place. Finally she brought herself to throw them out.

Gwenda ate half a piece of toast, without butter or jam. 'Have some more,' Ruth said. 'Or some cake. It's home-made. Or café-made, at least.'

'You should probably watch how much cake you eat,' said Gwenda. 'At your age.'

Ruth looked at the wall, counted the candles.

'Have you seen Caroline recently?' her mother went on. 'The way she's let herself go.'

Ruth frowned, thinking of her sister-in-law back in the

autumn. Caroline had put on weight. She'd worn the same dress every day, tight on the bust and arm, her hair loose, no make-up. She'd seemed relaxed, contented. That was good, Ruth had thought. At the same time, she couldn't understand how Caroline could just give up, sit down wherever she happened to be, her unflattering dress spread around her in the dirt.

'She wants to be careful,' said Gwenda. 'You can't expect a man to put up with that.'

Ruth pushed the plate of cake aside. 'So, do you feel up to another shop?'

'Can I help you?' The woman was dressed in delicate pale neutrals that would not stand the weather. The clothes and the designer silver at her neck said the shop was a hobby, something to do now that the children were gone. She had draped it with beautiful fabrics, whimsical jewellery, little scarves, belts, beaded purses. The women who came in were just like her. They applied themselves to the choices they had to make. They ran their fingers through the silks and cashmeres, held them to their faces, closed their eyes.

The woman's glance tracked over Gwenda. Ruth knew what she was seeing, the shoes, the trousers, the cheap handbag. Ruth spoke first. 'We'll just have a look around to start with,' she smiled. 'We want something for a special occasion. Something cosy. But luxurious.'

'Not too luxurious,' said Gwenda.

The woman looked at Ruth, costed her up. She nodded, afforded her a small smile. 'Of course,' she said. 'Just ask if you need any help.'

'I don't think we will,' said Gwenda, looking at the racks suspiciously.

'Thank you very much,' said Ruth, her biggest smile, a widening of her eyes: *I'm sorry, I'm doing my best, you know how it is.*

The woman's mouth twitched, acknowledging, conspiratorial. *Mothers,* her eyebrows said.

The woman could be Ben's mother, Ruth thought. A woman like her. She felt, suddenly, his hands on her, pressing on the small of her back, and turned away, her carefully chosen clothes all at once flimsy, transparent.

She followed her mother. Gwenda was moving down the racks, picking at the labels. 'Look at these prices,' she said.

'It's good quality,' said Ruth.

'I can't spend this sort of money on clothes.'

'Why not? What are you saving it for?'

'For you,' said Gwenda. 'You and Aled.'

'For goodness sake, Mother. You don't need to do that. Spend it on yourself.'

'Don't turn your nose up at it. A single woman your age. You could get ill, lose your job.'

'I'm insured against that.'

'Pfft.' Her mother pushed a hanger into line. 'Are you insured against getting old?'

Ruth flicked at a sleeve, let it fall.

'I know you think it won't happen,' her mother said. 'But it will. And no one to look after you.'

'I don't need looking after.'

Gwenda turned toward her. 'I worry about you, Ruthie.'

Ruth looked back at her. Down at her. Sometimes she forgot

how short Gwenda was. She let out a breath. 'There's no need to, Mum. Honestly. I've got everything under control.'

They stood like that, looking at each other, then Gwenda turned back to the clothes. 'You always did have to know best,' she said.

'We can't all be as easygoing as you,' said Ruth.

Gwenda laughed, a quick soft explosion that for a moment startled the fallen days from her face.

They kept moving towards the back of the shop. Ruth pulled out a hanger. 'What do you think of this?'

Her mother scarcely looked at it. 'Not for me.'

'This is nice.'

Gwenda snorted.

'What about this?' Ruth pulled out a long cardigan and dress in soft wool, a rich plum shade.

'Hmm,' said her mother, feeling the material. 'How much is it?'

'Why don't you just try it first?'

'It'll be too small for me.'

'Don't be ridiculous.'

'What shoes could I wear with it?'

'Your black boots.'

'Hmm.' But Gwenda's eyes had changed, she was seeing something distant, intangible, a vision of what she could be.

'Let's take it to the changing room,' said Ruth.

Gwenda was a very long time changing. 'Are you okay?' Ruth kept asking.

'Don't nag me,' said Gwenda.

'Oh,' said Ruth, when her mother came out. 'That's really nice.' She found she was surprised.

'Do you think so?' Gwenda smiled at her, uncertain, shy. 'Have a look.'

Gwenda stood in front of the tall mirrors. She turned sideways, back again. Ruth, standing behind her, could see what she was seeing. The cardigan fell in graceful folds from the bones of Gwenda's shoulders, her arms. The dress skimmed the flat place where her breasts had been, her hollow stomach, fell gently to mid calf. There was nothing to get in the way of the fabric. Nothing to spoil its line.

Gwenda looked at Ruth. She was smiling. 'It seems to fit. Imagine that.'

She looked back at herself and smiled again. She was finally what she should be. Her bones had risen from the unseemly flesh. This might be the first time in her whole life that she recognised the body in the mirror. The first time that she liked it.

Ruth, standing at her mother's shoulder, looked from Gwenda's reflection to her own. She tilted her head, touched her collar. The blouse was wrong, she thought. Too classic. Old-fashioned even. And this jacket wasn't quite the right cut. Something a little longer perhaps. Something more fitted around the waist. She twitched at it irritably.

All the long years of this yet to be gone through.

Gwenda was still looking at herself. She twirled gently. The fabric lifted then settled, weightless as a shadow flickering on a wall, a shadow rising and falling as someone passes, for a moment, before the light.

THE COMMUNION DRESS

✄

Claudia Rapport

She was short on sins. Again.

Soon it would be her turn. The church was cold. She hunched up her shoulders, wrapped herself a little tighter in her thick cardigan, rubbed her hands together, bowed her head and knelt on the cross-stitched prie-dieu of St George and the dragon, which looked a little tame and not worth slaying. She scribbled a few sinful ideas in her new notebook but none of them appealed: she had not killed anyone, and neither had she robbed or been violent. With no siblings to fight with, a mother who believed in unquestioning obedience and what Anne-Marie supposed was her own lack of imagination, she had never been tempted to do anything really bad. Which was why she needed another two sins to make it to seven, the number that, according to Father Dominique, was the minimum a good Catholic committed on a weekly basis.

She wondered why her friend Nicole was taking so long, and while she was waiting decided to pray to the Virgin Mary who looked bored and distant even though, sitting on her lap, baby Jesus was clapping his hands and wanting to play. Anna noticed that one of the Holy Mother's toes was chipped.

Her own feet were frozen and the pins and needles in her knees forced her back into a sitting position. Concerned she might make sense of the whisperings behind the heavy velvet curtains that hid priest and penitent, she slid along the pew and waited. Too late she realised that by staying where she was she could have accused herself of being nosy, that she had missed the opportunity of an extra sin.

She chewed the end of her pencil, doodled a few bell-skirted shapes on the blank page and let her thoughts turn to her First Communion dress: 'une création italienne', the manageress of Frank's had pointed out – *the specialist in women's and girls' fashion for the discerning.* 'Dearer than the others, of course, but it will stand out,' she'd assured Anne-Marie's mother, 'and think how proud you'll feel watching your daughter walking down the aisle.'

Pride, there was the sixth sin. It would have to do, as long as Father Dominique didn't force her to explain about the dress, which should have been delivered that afternoon while she was in school, two days late because, apparently, it had to be let out a little at the waist.

'That's as maybe,' she'd heard her mum tell Madame Lelong at the Boutique on the phone, 'but it's most inconvenient and I've had to rearrange my daughter's appointment with the photographer.'

Nicole's confession was over; she extricated herself from the over-carved mahogany booth, hung on each side with a moth-eaten velvet curtain, the colour of old port, walked past Anne-

Marie and winked, before kneeling by the altar in a pretence of contrition. According to Anne-Marie's father, Nicole's parents were non-believers, but if she were to be her grandmother's heir the child had to be brought up as a good Catholic. The way Nicole flirted with the boys at the Catechism classes Anne-Marie didn't think it was working, but she wouldn't tell on a friend.

Whenever Anne-Marie entered the gloomy confessional it was with a sense of foreboding. It was stuffy inside, dark, almost sinister, and every week she wondered what happened to sins once they had been formulated, worried she might be contaminated, even catch a mortal one.

'Don't be ridiculous,' her mother had said when Anne-Marie expressed her fear, 'concentrate on your transgressions, and in any case once absolution has been granted the sins have been wiped out.' Which seemed to Anne-Marie an easy way out, if not an invitation for sinners to do it all over again.

At least, protected by the latticework that separated her from Father Dominique she didn't have to look at the priest's face and could ignore his twitching left eye, which translated any inner turmoil with an increase in the frequency and force of the spasms.

'Forgive me father for I have sinned.' Back on her knees and no cross-stitched cushion this time to mediate between her flesh and the bare wood.

Behind the black grille the Priest bowed his white spectral head and cleared his throat. 'Well, Anne-Marie—'

She squirmed, closed her eyes and tightened her clasped fingers until they almost hurt. An all-knowing God was one thing, but that it should apply to Father Dominique could make church an uncomfortable place to be in, and even the most beautiful of dresses might not, she feared, make up for the way he had to stare and reproach.

'...let's hear your confession and hope you will be in a true state of grace when comes the time for you to receive our Lord.'

'Yes, Father.'

She unfolded her list of sins, and slowly, in the hope he would not notice she was one short, set to accusing herself of mild pilfering – a few centimes of left-over bread money; of answering back – not much, she would not dare risk the slipper; adding a hint of envy – her cousin didn't have to wear home-made clothes; a show of bad temper – she still thought justified; a little greed – three helpings of ice cream had been too much, and of course pride – the beautiful dress that would set her apart from the other forty-eight girls in her Communion class.

'I make it six, my child.'

'I can't think of anything else, Father.'

'Is that so? I trust you have given much thought to your confession on the eve of your Communion.'

'Yes, Father.'

'What about—' he paused for a few seconds, cleared his throat, 'what about bad thoughts, any of those in the last few days?'

What he meant by 'bad' she was not quite sure, but decided it might be safer not to antagonise him for fear he would launch into one of his long discourses on the importance of the purity of the soul, and the state of grace when about to receive the Host. 'I don't think so, Father.'

It was after he granted her absolution that he suggested she should come and see him after the final rehearsal later that afternoon, 'I won't keep you long. We must make sure you are truly worthy of our Lord, you do see that don't you?'

She disposed of the three 'Hail Marys' and two 'Our Fathers' of her penance, and remembered just in time to cross herself and dip into a slow genuflection before hurrying up the aisle, away from the presence of Jesus and the little orange light that burned on the altar.

Her mother, who must have been listening for the clanking of the lift, opened the door before Anne-Marie had time to ring the doorbell and failed, for once, to tell her off for putting the parquet floor at risk with her outdoor shoes.

'Better go and wash your hands.'

Anne-Marie even scrubbed her nails with the Sunday hard brush, dried each finger in turn on the clean towel, took a few deep breaths and made her way to the dining room. Her mother stood, as if to attention by the side of the oak table, its surface almost hidden by the largest cardboard box Anne-Marie had ever seen, as shiny as the white patent shoes they had chosen the week before.

Caught between the need to see and touch the dress, and the feeling that the anticipation should last longer – that here was a moment to be framed in her mind so as to remember it better – she stood, arms dangling by her side, and did nothing.

'It won't bite you know.' Her mother nudged her forward. Together they loosened the pale pink satin ribbon, freed the box and eased away the four corners of the lid. With extreme care, as if the contents might escape, or vanish, or turn out to be breakable, they raised the lid, and there, in front of them, lapped an undisturbed sea of white and pink tissue paper. Anne-Marie hesitated, looked up to seek her mother's approval, and on a nod, let her fingers plunge in and create whispering, rustling waves, until, in a final tide, she revealed the white Communion dress puffed up with scrunched up lengths of silky paper. Neither spoke. They stood and ran their eyes over the sweeping A line skirt, the tiny buttons – later Anne-Marie was to count fifty-four of them – as they cascaded from throat to foot, and the narrow stitched down horizontal pleats, almost rhythmic in the way they occurred every few centimetres or so, and reached down to the hem.

Anne-Marie watched her mother slide a careful hand under the bodice while the other snaked under the skirt. She lifted out the dress, and draped it over her outstretched arm. 'You'd better try it on, just to make sure,' to make sure of what she didn't say, 'and bring the underskirts, they should be at the bottom of the box. Don't forget the bonnet and the bag.' They processed down the narrow corridor that led to Anne-Marie's bedroom, and it was with the kind of tenderness she might have shown a sick child that her mother gathered the dress and laid it carefully over the narrow single bed.

Anne-Marie knelt down to stroke the dress. Never had she felt material so soft, so yielding yet strong and structured, nothing like the brown paper pattern pinned on her weeks ago in the boutique.

'It's organdie.' The word held wealth, elegance, and a hint of mystery.

Once she had taken off the navy skirt and pale blue blouse, Anne-Marie stood in the middle of the room in her everyday cotton pants and vest, stared at her feet, kicked off her shoes and waited. It would be years before she understood her mother's need to be the one to see her first, in the dress that so looked like a mini bridal outfit, to share the joy, but without the threat of a man's love about to steal her child from her.

With unhurried and purposeful gestures, as if she were remembering a ritual of old, mother presented daughter with the longsleeved under-dress of lawn cotton supposed to minimise any itching – and the risk of unsightly scratching during the ceremony. Anne-Marie slipped it over her head, closed her eyes, breathed in a mouthful of cloth, struggled to guide her arms down the narrow sleeves, and stood still while her mother tied the little satin ribbons at the back, to secure the dress in place. The short opening on the side made stepping inside the stiff underskirt awkward and Anne-Marie nearly lost her balance. 'It's like wearing a lampshade,' she said, wobbling.

The remark made them laugh, turned them into accomplices, dispelled the almost sombre mood of the moment.

Unlike a chrysalis which sheds the protective membrane it no longer needs before turning into a butterfly, with each layer she put on, Anne-Marie felt herself growing taller, more confident, almost elegant. The dress settled over her body with ease, and she let her mother adjust the waist, button up the cuffs, smooth down the skirts, and tie up the belt in a bow at the back. 'Let's have a look at you.' Her mother nudged her towards the mirror and, eyes half-closed, Anne-Marie prayed the reflection would match the image she had put together. It did. Only to be spoilt by the tight-fitting bonnet which crushed her blond curls, emphasised the plumpness of her cheeks, and was only just redeemed by the organdie veil that reached the middle of her back.

Her mother stood behind her so that the mirror encompassed them both, the picture broken almost as soon as it formed. 'What time do you have to be back for the final rehearsal?' She tweaked at the skirt, puffed up the veil, stood back and clucked her approval. 'Very nice—' she said it a couple of times. 'Make sure you come straight home when it's over, time for you to have a bath and wash your hair.'

On the church steps Nicole pulled Anne-Marie by the sleeve, 'Hurry up! Father Dominique is on the war path; apparently we are going to be short of candles for the procession. He's in a right state!'

Inside they nearly collided with a vase of tall lilies in the hands of an elderly woman scuttling towards the altar of St Antoine. The girls hurried down the long row of straw-covered chairs to take up their places, pulled out their rosaries, put their hands together and muttered what might have been prayers under their breath, while the organist tried to overcome a sticky patch of the 'Ave Maria'.

Cassock flapping, Father Dominique came storming out of the sacristy and stood at the foot of the main altar. The class of 1956 fell silent.

'Let's go through the procession once more. No dragging of feet,' he turned to the boys, 'and look ahead, not at your parents.' That was for the girls. 'There'll be plenty of time when the service is over for smiles and compliments. Is that clear?'

'Yes, Father.' Seventy thin young voices harmonised as one. In twos they walked up and down the nave, the girls first, counting the number of steps under their breath, followed by the boys, a little gauche and, Anne-Marie reflected, unlikely to be looking forward to having to wear their first best suit in the morning, even if it meant long trousers.

'Remember what an honour it is for the Parish to have our Bishop with us tomorrow. I expect you to be on best behaviour.' He stared at two of the boys who were making faces at each other. 'For those of you who will receive the Host from his Grace, make sure you cast your eyes down as a mark of respect.'

'Yes, Father.'

'Do not forget that the fast begins at eight.' There were a few moans. 'Save me the grumbling. Remember what our Lord suffered for us on the cross.'

At last it was over. The organ blew out a last chord, excited children bade each other good night, doors clanked shut, lights went off and Anne-Marie thought he had forgotten about her when his voice called out from a dark corner. 'Anne-Marie, just a moment please.'

She had been in the sacristy before but never on her own, and there was something uncomfortable about the smell of incense, burnt-out candles and decaying flowers.

'I won't keep you long, I promise.' She wondered if he could read her mind. 'Sit in front of me so that I can see you properly.' He moved his chair so close she felt his liquorice breath on her face. 'Now, if I recall correctly we were to discuss these bad thoughts of yours.' His eye twitched, closed, twitched again, faster this time.

She lowered her gaze, rested it on a large darning spot on the skirt part of his soutane.

'Of course I am very concerned.' He spired his hands together, aligned them against his mouth, and bowed his head a little.

'Well,' she began, 'actually, I—' She considered explaining to him about lying about the seventh sin just to make up the numbers, but he gave her no time.

He released his hands, stretched out the right one and rested it on her thigh. 'Now, tell me, about these thoughts of yours.'

His fingers pressed a little harder.

'There is nothing to be afraid of my child, you and I know each other well, don't we?'

She nodded.

'I would like you to think of me as a friend, an older friend obviously but one who might help you grow up into a fine young woman.' His lips looked flush with blood. 'You do understand what I mean don't you, my child?'

She was not sure she did, but said yes because that was what he must have been expecting of her.

His fingers crawled up, stopped, retreated and this time it was under the navy skirt that they settled, burning tips on her cold flesh. They would not stay still, they rubbed and pressed and crept higher. He had almost reached the small ridge of elastic of her underpants. She pressed her thighs together, looked past his shoulders, sought help from the Virgin smiling down on her from a flaky oil painting.

A loud knock on the door and Nicole burst in.

'Sorry to interrupt, Father—' she smiled as if there was nothing incongruous about the priest's hand on her friend's thigh, 'but I was sent to tell you that the extra candles have just been delivered. I thought you'd be pleased. Come on,' she reached out for Anne-Marie's hand, 'better be on our way.' She walked a few steps, turned round and delivered a brisk 'Goodnight, Father,' before hurrying out of the room.

'I was wondering if Old Greasy Paws was going to have a go at you. He likes them a little plump and innocent. No luck with me. Told him I'd speak to my parents about him, not that I would,' she laughed. 'They might not believe me but he can't take the risk.'

'My mother would if I told her.' With fingers that shook, Anne-Marie smoothed her skirt down and blushed at the thought of the creeping hand.

'Just make sure you're never alone with him. See you in the morning.' She set off, turned round and laughed, 'As long as we look the part who cares?'

Anne-Marie did.

It was a subdued child her mother welcomed home with the news that her godmother had brought a very special gift. 'I think it's the watch you were hoping for.'

'That's nice.'

'Is that all you've got to say?'

Anne-Marie shrugged her shoulders, and made her way to the bathroom. She locked herself in, finding it hard to believe that her shame didn't show when she looked at herself in the mirror.

She didn't sleep very much that night, kept waking on the edge of nightmares where hands turned to rats and scuttled all over her body, and when the light of dawn filtered through the closed shutters she stared miserably at the ghostly communion dress which now looked like a shroud.

MADE IN WALES

✂

Daisy Golding

I am the fashion police – that is in so far as I can make or break
one of those silly girls who think they're an actress/singer or
model/presenter. What do I do? I write a column in one of the
Matalan-does-Prada handbag weeklies. You know the kind of
thing, costs a quid or two, full of fat women, thin-to-the-point-
of-emaciation skinny women and girls who don't even know
their own names any more thanks to the champagne and coke…
I thought it would be fun, but now it's not. I've seen one too
many of them crack under the strain of too many lovers and
late nights, too many crotch shots as they exit black cabs and
stretch limos. I used to think I could write, that I'd be a hot
shot investigative journalist…like the guys I met a lifetime
ago, when I was temping for a publisher intent on beating an
injunction on a book written by *The Sunday Times* Insight team.
It was about some dubious political goings-on to do with the
Masons and their funny handshake friends. Now I'm not so
sure; the big novel languishes in a suitcase under the spare bed

and my home computer gathers dust and cat hair in a corner of the living room.

Daytimes I sleep, waiting for the alarm to ring at about two and raise me from dreams of another life and another place (where I've got two smiley ginger-nut children and a Scottish hubby who's retired from his ambition to be a popstar and settled for millionaire kitchen company ownership, but that's another story...). At three I leave the confines of my hard-fought-for attic in Soho for the office – it's not far, I can walk it in twenty minutes, could cycle it in ten if I had somewhere to keep a bike. Then it's down to business, sorting through the newspaper clippings and the newsfeed clicker that constantly buzzes with tips coming in from LA and New York, and, given it's August, shots from beaches on the Med that the D-listers thought might just be under the paparazzi's radar.

It's not that I don't like these girls, they're trying to make a living too, but I don't like what they and their fans have turned me into. I'm a vampire living off their vanity, sucking up to their fans' desire for insights into a life they want but can't have; exposing the frailties of those who have dared to grab a chance at the limelight, at their five minutes of fame. Writing about the boyfriends and the diets, the handbags and the hairdos just keeps the whole damned circus going. I don't like them and I don't like me. I even read the wretched mags when I get home, terrified that someone else might pick up on a story I've missed, a new face that I hadn't spotted at the latest booze fest of a perfume launch.

It all started to go downhill about six months ago when I gave up freelance fashion journalism – I'd begun to disturb my regular editors with a number of increasingly righteous 'think pieces' regarding the evils of bling. Pressure from the mortgage and impending credit crunch meant taking just whatever I could get and this was the first thing that came up and paid the requisite amount. To be honest, I'm a bit long in the tooth for it really but they'd tried a neophyte just out of Central St Martin's and that hadn't worked, so they were prepared to give a slightly wrinkled, forty-something has-been a go.

I like writing; I like clothes; once upon a time I even liked writing about clothes, despite the original ambitions to out-Paxman the best of them – but now it just seems like I'm adding to the world's ills. I truck my stuff in jeans and Converse, trying not to look too much like mutton dressed…or a shorter, fatter Janet Street Porter. The younger girls seem to think I'm okay, in a 'we'll tolerate her so long as she doesn't gatecrash too many parties or mother my boyfriend' kind of way. Or at least they did for a while. Now I'm not so sure. The late nights and hard partying seem to be buffing up my acerbic buttons, so that chummy sincerity is getting harder to find.

It was that last trip to Milan that did it. Perhaps insisting on going by train, and putting in the exorbitant travel expenses that went with it, was taking it a bit far. Then again maybe not, maybe it was trying to push too many other people's buttons. I used to be funny, but the joke's wearing thin. The show was Dai Martin's – his first on the continent, outside of his English-speaking comfort zone. A Brit five years out of art school and flying high on a tide of Vivienne Westwood meets Marc Jacobs – all tartan gothic and pared-down tailoring. Dai had been an early spot of mine, before he got all camped up and giggly.

I couldn't help myself. Once he'd told me that I was his

muse – despite my lack of stature and chest – that having read my infrequent but spiky pieces for an upmarket broadsheet he'd had the guts to get up off his Ponty estate sofa and try for the dream his comprehensive school careers master had laughed out of court. (He'd suggested instead that the poor lad look for something in the local knicker factory.) Said it was something about learning that ordinary people have dreams that are realisable, if only they have the gumption to see that boundaries are set by the insecure whose own dreams have turned to dust. Must have looked me up and found we'd been born only 20 miles or so from each other and that, therefore, getting out of the land of slag heaps and chapel on Sundays was possible after all – even with only two crap 'A' levels to one's name. Now he was up to something I couldn't quite put my finger on, but I knew his latest press release didn't ring true, that he wouldn't have chosen to launch in Italy given a choice—

Dai Martin will launch his collection 'My Kind of Town' at the Palazzo del Amitri on 23 March 2007. You are kindly invited to attend. RSVP.

Short but sweet. I hadn't expected an invite, one of the year's golden tickets, I wasn't exactly front-row material. Why might I have suddenly popped back onto the database I wondered. Still, getting to talk to fellow front-rowers might give me the inside track on the European move and what it meant for Dai. I might even get to chat to the man himself. (Some hope.)

*

I made sure she was on the list. There was no way I could do anything else. I needed to get the message back 'ome. There was no way they would understand otherwise. It's not just about the money – it's about trying to change things, trying to do my bit, payback time. It seemed only fair, because I truly believe that without her example I'd never have made it over the Severn Bridge. Me mam and dad did the best they could, but it's not easy when you lose your job, the only one you've ever 'ad, and your kids are all under ten. When you'll never work again 'cause of the bad chest and your eldest son announces that he's a big girl's blouse and wants to go to art college and do fashion.

Fashion – what's that when it's at 'ome, it's not a job, it's not even an 'obby, boy, it's for girls…hey, you're not tellin' me you're one of them, are you, boy? Not that. I know you've never liked the rugby, put it down to you bein' a bit on the small side, but you were quite happy to come down to Sophia Gardens and watch Glamorgan in the summer, even watch a bit of footie on the box—

No, I'm not gay, just not interested really, boys or girls, never 'ad the time. It's more about making everyone look their best, feel good about themselves, make the best of themselves. 'Cause we are all good enough. Doesn't matter where you went to school, or whether you speak French or Sais or Cymraeg, even Italian – or what bloody colour your skin is. That's what it's always been about, that's why she was so important to me. Gave me something to aim for, a link with the big time, a way out. I worked me ass off, mind, just to make sure it happened. Anyhow, tonight's the night. Work's done; girls – no bleedin' skin an' bone either, got that in the contract too, I want something real up there, not a photographer's wet dream that makes the drape look better – dressers, hair guys, make-up mavens, they're all here. And there's Gianina…yeah, yeah, I know, I'm a great big sell-out. But there are some things you can't do without the really big bucks, an' I just ain't there yet. Probably never woulda been—

You see, it's not just about her, the journalist, it's about loads of blokes like me dad, lads like me, girls like our Rhian; I just wanted her to have the exclusive, give something back. 'Cause I know she needs it, and I know how to do it, and it's a real good feeling to be able to do it. It was one of the things I made sure was in the contract. No way was I gonna sign it if not. Not for any money, 'cause I said, didn't I, 's not about the money, 's about home, saying ta very much, 'cause I appreciate it. I'm gonna make it, dim prob, and I want 'em all to know why and how. See, I've cleared it with the boss, I've told her that I'm all hers, but only on my terms—

There's my tune, Bonnie Tyler, cheesy I know, but we'll finish with Cerys, just to up me cred' a teensy bit. It'll only be an hour or so an' they'll all know something's up. S'pose someone in Ponty knows, they must, but they'll be bein' paid well to keep it shut. They don't wanna be the odd one out, the biggest loser, now do they?

Shh…gotta listen now and see if they're clappin'…nice… oohs an' aah's where there should be. And Gianina's stopped pacin' an' is lightin' up again, so she must be okay with it. Bloody stuffed if she's not, 'cause she can still sack me, despite me puttin' all that stuff in the contract, the designs 'ave still got to work. We gotta sell 'em and sell 'em by the lorry-load – see 'em ripped off down the markets in Merthyr and Milan an' everywhere in between. Bit nicer imitations in Matalan and

Tesco, so the girls I went to school with can wear 'em, too. Right, gotta go now. Get ready to roll, make that announcement, share it with the world, well some of it anyhow, keep the exclusive for me inspiration. Here comes the boss…gonna do it together, me an' Gianina, that'll show em back in Ponty. Me all over the glossies, but headlines in the *Western Mail*, too, that'll make a change, eh? Don't s'pose Gianina's been on the front page in the *South Wales Argus* before either, so it'll be a first for her! Bet 'er mam'll put that in 'er scrapbook, too.

*

So, I booked the train – one for the bods in Corporate Social Responsibility to argue over with Accounts: environmental sustainability versus financial sustainability; should keep them busy for months arguing that one out – and I booked the hotel, small but central, cheaper than some but not terribly cheerful. Then, on the big night I ate early and made damn sure I was on time. What was odd wasn't that I wasn't front row – didn't expect to be really – but that I was right by the top left-hand bit of the T of the runway and at the bottom of a set of steps leading up to the stage. It started with Bonnie Tyler – my god, what was he trying to say? I know the 80s and shoulder pads are due a revival, but Bonnie? The clothes were good, though, very, very good. Then I began to take in a few of the faces around me, not just the usual independents but some big industry movers and shakers, and mostly from the one fashion house or its overseas outposts; they couldn't be scouting, they'd have been spotted and anyway their big couture show had been and gone. Then the evening wear was over and Cerys was fading into the background. On he came, Dai, to a standing ovation, mincing his way over from the other side of the T, a very familiar figure at his side. So that was it, he'd sold his soul to one of the biggest names in the game, given away his independence to bankroll a collection that was good, but maybe not great. And how much of it was his, undiluted, I couldn't help but wonder. It made me sick to the soles of my rhinestone baseball boots. All that pushing and shoving to make his way up the ladder, flogging himself and his devoted team to within an inch of their lives and for what? For a big fat cheque from a big fat Italian company with a vacuum at its heart. I couldn't stand it – from balls to bling in less than a season – with anger in my heart and fire in my soul I pushed my way back through the still-applauding crowd and headed off to file my broadsheet copy, righteousness at the ready.

That was it. My big mistake. Not waiting around to see what the boy wonder had to say for himself. The scoop of a lifetime lost and the editor furious, P45 in the post. Because less than two minutes after I left the building, Dai, when the crowd had quieted enough to let him be heard, made his big announcement and I should have been part of it. He thanked Gianina for her faith and generosity, called out for me (apparently gutted at finding the seat at the foot of the steps empty, when he came to grab me by the hand), and told the standing masses that this collection would be designed in Italy but made in Wales – guaranteeing jobs for the 250 workers who thought they'd be losing them when another house moved their production to Eastern Europe a couple of weeks before. That he wasn't going to say more than that, except as an exclusive to the journalist who had given his ambition a launch pad and would she please join them on the runway. Of course, when the muse couldn't be found – because she was already phoning in her diatribe about the British sell-out afraid to go with the courage of his convictions – he had to say something, Gianina wouldn't settle for waiting, not with *Vogue* and *Women's Wear Daily* on the edge of their seats. After all, she'd given Dai and me our chance, our moment. Big business can't wait on no-shows.

The moral of the story being never assume the worst. Not everyone's dreams are soured by experience. Some kids do come good and stay good. They're not all changed by the bright lights and the big time, some of them do remember where they came from and why hard work matters. That there is satisfaction in the day-to-day graft and pride to be had in a job well done, no matter how lowly. Not every Katie wants to be a Jordan, nothing sacred if it gets five minutes more airtime.

So here I am, doing the night shift and learning hard lessons. I think maybe it's time for a change. To give something back, just like Dai. Only this time it needs to be real, tangible, a million miles from New York and London, Paris and Milan. A flyer fell out of the last *Marie Claire* I filched from the office – VSO, in Africa. Not sure what I could do for them but apparently some of the smaller NGOs are always looking for English teachers, for the kids who walk five miles to school in holey cast-offs from First World doorstep collections. If nothing else, it would be a welcome break from China White and chilled champagne…

A WOMAN OF GRACE

✂

Suzy Ceulan Hughes

Grace had not married for love. She had married Archibald for his name. Oh, good gracious, no – not the Archibald bit. That was ghastly. It was his surname that she wanted, and the only way she could see of getting it was by being his wife. Grace Darling. Darling, Grace. Darling Grace. She felt she had become herself, the person she was always meant to be. It was a name that made her feel loved.

Most people were puzzled by the marriage, though far too polite to say so. Some of Archibald's male friends, however, could quite understand why he had proposed to Grace, but they were not about to say so to their wives.

'Can *you* see what he sees in her, George?' Phyllis asked her husband on the way home from a dinner party a few weeks before the wedding. 'She seems rather vulgar and superficial to me. And she really has no conversation. Joan and I were chatting away about the children as usual and we tried ever so hard to include Grace, but she didn't seem at all interested, even though she's about to get married. All she wanted to talk about was *Vogue* and *Harper's Bazaar* and that Italian woman. What's her name? Schiaparelli, I think it is. I suppose that explains the ridiculous dress she was wearing tonight. I'm really not sure about the decency of exposing quite so much flesh, even if it is the height of fashion. Or was, I should say. She must have been frozen. I really don't know what dear Archie is thinking of.'

'I suppose she is rather beautiful,' said George.

George had taken Grace's coat when she and Archie had arrived at the restaurant that evening. As he had slipped the coat from Grace's shoulders, he had found himself gazing at her gloriously naked back. He had noticed a small mole to the right of her spine, low down, just above the edge of the black satin that sheathed her hips and shimmered around her legs as she moved.

Phyllis sighed loudly.

'I sometimes think men are terribly shallow and short-sighted,' she said. 'The fact that a woman is attractive hardly means she's going to be a good wife. Or mother, for that matter. Quite the opposite, in fact.'

'Oh, I don't know about that, dear,' said George. 'And I see no reason why a man shouldn't want to have an attractive wife on his arm.'

'Whatever do you mean, George?' said Phyllis. 'You mean, like some sort of accessory?'

'No, no, dear, you misunderstand me,' said George. 'What I mean is— Well, you're beautiful and I think you're a wonderful wife.'

George realised he was blustering now and wondered whether

he would get away with it.

'Oh, thank you, darling,' said Phyllis.

She reached across to put her right hand on George's leg and kept it there, her fingers gently stroking his inner thigh, until they reached home.

The wedding was a small, quiet affair, with Archibald's friends and their wives, girlfriends or fiancées accounting for most of the congregation at the church and the invitees at the wedding breakfast afterwards. Archibald was an only child and both his parents had died fairly recently. Grace's family, what little of it there was apparently, lived in Wiltshire – too far away to make the journey up to town, Grace had explained. She and Archibald would visit them as part of their honeymoon and celebrate with them that way, she had told Phyllis. But there was a belated change of plan and the couple spent their honeymoon in quite another part of the country. And, very soon after their return, Grace discovered that she was pregnant.

'She says,' Phyllis told George, 'that Dr Scot has advised her against travelling any distance. Which seems odd, since he told *me* to carry on as normal when I was expecting Elizabeth.'

'Perhaps she doesn't have your strong constitution, darling,' said George.

'She looks perfectly strong enough to me,' said Phyllis.

And Grace did seem to bloom during each of her pregnancies, delivering three healthy infants – a girl and two boys – in rapid succession.

'She says the chloroform is marvellous,' Phyllis told George. 'But when I asked her if she was breastfeeding this time, she said giving birth was quite enough of an ordeal, without having to spend months with an infant chewing at her breast. And she wants to get her figure back as quickly as possible, though I can't imagine why. It's not as though it matters once you're settled. As long as you're happy. Other things are so much more important than keeping your looks. Don't you think, George?'

'I'm sure you're right, dear,' said George, looking at his wife over the top of the *Telegraph*. Phyllis had become quite plump. The Mediterranean blood showing through, thought George. But, for the same reason, she still had that lovely olive complexion, with the brown eyes and a mass of dark curls that she had recently started brushing into the long, smooth bob that was all the rage and that George hated. Ah well, you can't have everything, thought George. And he did love her so. It was a shame she had never softened towards Grace. He knew Archie was giving her a hard time but did not like to mention it to his wife. Phyllis had always liked Archibald and he did not want to disillusion her. And Archie was one of his oldest friends. But George knew his discretion was not just about protecting Phyllis or Archie. It was about respecting Grace's privacy. He felt she was entitled to that.

'There's something very strange about that woman,' said Phyllis over supper one evening. 'She sent one of the boys round today to borrow a piece of steak. How can you "borrow" a piece of steak? And what good is one piece of steak to an entire family, I ask you?'

'Perhaps she hadn't bought enough,' said George. 'It's an easy enough mistake, I'm sure.'

'Don't be silly, George,' said Phyllis. 'A woman knows how much steak she needs to make a meal. I was tempted to refuse but when I asked Philip what his mother was cooking he came over all shy, which isn't like him at all. He looked as though he was about to cry, so I just sent him home with the steak. It all seemed very odd.'

'I'm sure it's nothing to worry about, dear,' said George, 'but you could always pop round to see her. They're only round the corner and we haven't seen them since the Mayor's Ball, which was weeks ago.'

George remembered seeing Archie and Grace arrive that evening. Unlike Phyllis, Grace had seemed to become ever more beautiful over the years and Archie had changed almost beyond recognition. His business had thrived, not despite but because of the war, and the rather dour and dowdy Archie that George remembered from before had become a sharp businessman with a dressing room full of tailor-made suits, soft linen shirts and handmade shoes of the finest leather. Grace, of course, had always known how to make the best of herself and they made a handsome couple now, knowing how to spend their money with taste and style and not a little glamour. For the ball, Grace had worn silk of the palest ice-pink, with a mink stole lined in the same colour. Her blonde hair had been pulled back into a neat chignon, and a beauty spot had been carefully placed to highlight perfect cheekbones. She had looked fabulous that night, and George had told Archie so.

'Oh, it's like having a fine painting,' Archie had said. 'You stop noticing it after a while.'

George had started to laugh before he realised Archie was not joking.

'And, in the end, you tire of it altogether,' Archie went on. 'It's very easy to dispose of a painting. If it's a good one, you might even get a return on your investment. It's a different matter with a wife.'

He had smiled then and George thought that perhaps he *was* joking after all.

'The boys are old enough to be sent away to school now. And I'll let Georgina go with her, of course, as part of the deal, so to speak,' said Archie. 'It would make life easier, anyway. I'll have the boys to follow me into the business when they're old enough, and a girl isn't much use in our trade, really. You can hire a secretary so cheaply these days.'

'But, Archie,' said George, 'you make your entire family sound like a business transaction.'

'Yes,' said Archibald. 'I suppose I do.'

When Phyllis knocked on the door, it was the nanny who answered.

'Mrs Darling is in the dressing room,' she said. 'Would you like to go on up?'

Phyllis had never been invited upstairs before and it took her a little while to find the right room. Grace was standing in front of a large wardrobe, with her back to the door. Phyllis could see that she had a pair of scissors in her hand and watched as she took a pair of trousers from their hanger, cut off one of the legs and dropped the pieces to the floor. Phyllis saw now that there was already a considerable pile of trousers at Grace's feet, all presumably with one leg removed.

'Grace, whatever are you doing?' said Phyllis.

'I am,' said Grace, 'cutting one leg off every pair of Archie's trousers. I've never done anything like this before, Phyllis, and perhaps I'll regret it. It does seem rather petty and spiteful. But I had to do something, just one small thing before I left. It's only his pride and his pocket that'll be hurt, after all.'

Grace turned to look at Phyllis. Her face was very pale, apart from a large bruise around her left eye, which was badly swollen.

'Oh, Grace,' said Phyllis. 'I'm so sorry. I never realised—'

'It's all right, Phyllis,' said Grace. 'It's over now, anyway. Archie wants a divorce. He says I've been a great asset to him but that it's time for us to go our separate ways. The boys are to stay with him. Georgina will be coming with me, though I'm not at all sure where we'll go. Back to Wiltshire, perhaps. Or to Canada. I hear Canada's splendid with opportunities – for women as well as for men. You were right all along, Phyllis. Archie and I should never have married. But I do wish you and I might have been friends, all the same. There was nothing for you to be jealous of, you see, nothing at all.'

THE WHITE SANDALS

✄

Sue Fortune

Most of the others had them, the girls who giggled in clusters in the playground, who played jacks deftly and skipped without tripping, and knew the words to the counting-out rhymes that excluded the unwanted from games or secrets.

My mother said I never *should*…and their green and white checked skirts flew graceful and swift as the white-sandal-shod feet cracked down, never missing a beat. White sandals, with two straps across their feet, socks open to the air at toe and heel. Her best friend in class, Jackie, had them, and so did Fiona-next-door.

Kitty, a sceptical and unprepossessing six-year-old with a short straight bang of hair the colour of cold tea, wore sensible brown Bata sandals, robust and round-toed, with a tasteful cut-out stamped as unobtrusively as possible on each foot. She was consulted to the extent that they should fit correctly, and Mummy liked the shop assistant to bring a few pairs to try on, to make quite sure they did. Kitty had long since given up expressing her preferences with any conviction on occasions like these because it would only lead to a ruined afternoon, with Mummy striking or shouting at her. She was simply issued with footwear, as the Joneses had been issued with Married Quarters, mosquito nets, cholera jabs.

Mummy thought the stiff Bata shoes (why 'sandals'? Surely *proper* sandals were less solid) were smart enough, though of course At Home it would have been Clarks. But you couldn't get Clarks in Singapore. 'Clarks are grown out before they're worn out,' Granny was quoted as saying, whenever the mothers discussed buying children's shoes. If outgrown shoes could be discarded while they still had some wear in them, it meant something. It was worth letting people know. Even Kitty could see that.

But the other girls' white sandals looked so lovely and cool. As cool as flip-flops, and much smarter. You couldn't wear flip-flops to school or Church. So in fact the white sandals were sensible. She had once said so in a shoe shop, but to her surprise Mummy had snapped, 'Certainly not. Horrid common things. Now hurry up and try these on. We haven't got all day.'

But while it hadn't occurred to Kitty that having similar footwear could make her similar to the other girls (a wish unvoiced and unexamined), she was no fool, and knew that if Helen Croft, whose father was the headmaster, wore them, white strappy sandals were unlikely to be a sure sign of horrid commonness.

The little girls then were not overly interested in glamour. One girl she knew had a Sindy doll, but Kitty felt dolls were rather pointless. All you did was put their clothes on. You couldn't cuddle and confide in them, like Teddy and Figaro the Cat and Yow-Yow the Bear. She was indifferent to her doll, an unlovable bride with curly golden hair and sharp red-tipped fingers which got caught on its lace sleeves. The doll was supposed to be a grown-up, so it had two rigid cones for a bosom. Kitty supposed Mummy must be like that under her clothes. She wasn't unkind to the doll, but she didn't mind three-year-old Brian playing with it, and tearing the lace sleeves on its talons.

She really preferred to go looking for tadpoles or to the comic exchange with Fiona-next-door or Jackie. Or hide in a shady bedroom with an Enid Blyton from the school library, or Hilda Boswell's *Fairy Tales*. Daddy didn't like people spending the daytime in bedrooms, and it was best not to read in the sitting room, where she would irritate Mummy and be told, 'Go out to play, for heaven's sake. You've always got your nose in a book. You'll wear specs when you grow up.' So she would sprawl on her tummy on the cool red tiles on the verandah. The Hilda Boswell's creamy cover had a soft dappled overlay of crimson polish from the tiles, as comforting and familiar as Teddy's bald patches. She'd read the stories dozens of times, sympathising with little Tom Thumb hiding crossly in his dolls' house from the nosy courtiers peering in inquisitively, or the poor Beast pining for his Beauty. Or she might luxuriate in the *Princess Pony Book*, memorising, without trying, 'Tom had a little pony, Jack' and 'A Highwayman came riding, riding, riding…' or *Alice in Wonderland*, (what *was* a Mock Turtle, a March Hare?).

Outside she would speculate about the chrysalids, fat as her fist, suspended in a sheltered place under the guttering near the kitchen door; high out of reach and inexplicably sinister, doing nothing but wait. They were reputed to have something to do with the black butterflies (or were they moths?), as broad as her two open hands, which sometimes took refuge between Mummy's nested rosewood tables in the dining room, dusty and feathered as small birds. Although these were not fearsome, there was something untrustworthy about the chrysalids. They were too still, the opposite of butterflies. They never came or went, but simply hung there waiting as if they were dead.

Kitty prowled the garden, spying on beetles and mantises. Nice Kano, the gardener, cut the pineapple from its nest of razor-sharp spines when it was ripe so the Joneses could have it after dinner. The leathery, needle-tipped rosette, with its secret tawny fruit at the centre, lurked in a gloomy corner where the kampong cat which kept the mice down (and occasionally gave birth in the airing cupboard, whence all but one kitten mysteriously vanished while the children were in bed) retired with unfortunate small birds. Kano once brought a live chicken in a cardboard box as a Christmas present. Kitty wished they could keep it – surely it would lay eggs, which would be useful as well as interesting – but knew better than to say so, and ate Francie's nasi goreng without fuss.

Sometimes ants formed a two-lane highway right through the house, one line returning, with crumbs put out to feed birds on the back lawn, to their ant city buried under a crack in the culvert at the front.

In the afternoons Flow-ar (that was Mummy's name for him, because it was what he called as he cycled around the houses) slowly did the rounds with his bike laden with tiger orchids and lilies to sell to the ladies of the camp. Most evenings the ice cream van would arrive with lollies for five cents. When the Joneses sat down to their tea, chik-chaks would run up the walls and over the ceiling, little lizards racing their own shadows. Each morning the first thing the children heard was the loud drone of the machine the Malayan man who sprayed the monsoon ditches with white billowing clouds of DDT, to keep the mosquitoes down, carried on his back. It left a smell which lingered for an hour or so, hanging on the morning air until the sun burnt it away or a monsoon washed everything clean with startling suddenness, as if abruptly impatient with how dusty it had all become.

Kitty wandered about the sultry camp – it was perfectly safe, with a perimeter fence and guardrooms. The streets were lined with enormous trees, which cast deep shade so you walked into a dense pool, cool as water, and then there was a small shock as you emerged into the dry burning sunshine beyond and then another as you plunged into the next shadow.

But she had a kind of idea that outside the camp wasn't so safe and pleasurable. On bus stops, when they went shopping, she saw posters with a picture of a bundle of sticks and the words UNITY IS STRENGTH written underneath, and then different writing, some curved and ornate with hooks and dots everywhere; some, which was Chinese, made of boxes and branches and curls. She thought they were like little forests grown from different types of trees.

And something called a *Stand-by* sometimes happened, which meant you got a day off school, and was something to do with the piles of sandbags which appeared by the roadsides. Even the wildest children were never tempted to run or jump on the sandbags. There was something altogether too serious about them, though none of them knew quite what.

And someone mentioned *Rioting* to Mummy, but when Kitty asked what it meant she was told she shouldn't be listening to grown-ups talking. She couldn't help hearing, though. She didn't listen on purpose, because it was her policy to do what she was supposed to do – be good at reading and sums and leave Mummy in peace to read *Woman's Journal* in the lounge or enjoy ginantonic with the other mothers by the swimming pool. Doing what you were supposed to meant not getting hit or shouted at.

You were supposed, if possible, to be pretty, she knew that, and knew she was not. She had come across a character described as 'plain' in a book, and asked Mummy what it meant, and was told 'Well, not ugly exactly. Like you.' Her hair was not golden, and it was dead straight. The Hilda Boswell princesses were all beautiful and had golden curls, except for Snow White and Elise, whose hair was coal-black to show off their delicate white skin. Mummy had golden curls. That was probably why she took such a long time in the hairdressers, while Kitty required only a Quick Trim. 'Just a Quick Trim for Kitty, please, and I'll make an appointment for Thursday afternoon.' Kitty's shorn head always looked darker after a haircut had taken away the top layers that were bleached by the sun. It was funny – the opposite of what happened to your skin. After the initial painful few weeks on the island, burnt scarlet and tender as the inside of a strawberry (a fruit unheard-of in Singapore), Kitty, like every other child in the camp, had been tanned almost as brown as her shoes.

In the mornings the girls wore green checked cotton frocks to school, but arriving home at lunchtime the children discarded clothes and shoes and tore around like savages in their pants, the sun baking hard into their bare shoulders. Even flip-flops were flung anyhow in a corner, as the children leapt monsoon ditches, scrambled up trees or booted a ball across the lawn. At bathtime Kitty's soles were grass-green, although after dusk, when frogs and toads came out from the monsoon ditches to sit on the tarmac in the finally bearable cool of the evening, Kitty would put her flip-flops back on. She took seriously the risk of stepping on one; could not bear to let her imagination dwell on the horror of it happening *with bare feet*. Paddling, too, in the brownish shallows at the yacht club, meant flip-flops. It wasn't just the thought of water snakes, but the whole hideous notion of soft creeping slimy things under her bare feet, lurking in the muddy sand and clinging, adherent strips of weed.

Mummy sometimes wore flip-flops, black or white leather with a golden trim and hard soles. She didn't wear them much because she liked to wear stockings. Sometimes Kitty would put them on for a game and go clacking absurdly over the red verandah tiles with the soles sticking out miles behind her tough little heels, until told sharply by Mummy to desist. Daddy too had flip-flops, giant versions of the children's rubber ones, but he seldom wore them. Mostly they came in handy for hitting the children when they irritated him.

Francie made special dresses for Mummy to wear at Ladies' Nights in the Mess, from special materials like *chiffon* or *brocade*. Kitty liked the names, said them softly to herself while she looked inside Mummy's wardrobe (she was not allowed to touch) at the dresses and high-heeled shoes, and snuffed the mysterious smells of scent and hairspray and nail varnish, which, even for a six-year-old savage like Kitty, were alluring.

But for herself she was largely indifferent to clothes. She

retained a pleasant memory of the nice crunkly feeling of a stiffened petticoat under a party dress, and the luxury of an angora bolero, which she had worn for Brian's Christening in England, but she had only worn them once, because they were Too Good.

For parties now Kitty had a blue nylon party dress, with frills. Some girls had magicians or snake charmers at their parties, but Helen Croft, the headmaster's daughter, had Fancy Dress, and everyone was invited. Kitty knew Mummy wouldn't like the idea of Fancy Dress, so she suggested that she could go as a fairy, and that would mean she could wear the blue dress. Mr Jones made a wand by fastening a silver foil-covered cardboard star to a cane; no one said anything about wings, which were clearly impractical and far too much trouble. Kitty, who had at no point entertained any particular wish to be a fairy, knew that all this was only an apology for fancy dress, and cared little for authenticity. But she was pretty sure that, wings or no wings, no fairy ever wore heavy, sensible brown sandals.

Kitty and Brian had learned to keep out of Mr Jones's way; it was easy to annoy him. But sometimes he came home large and loud and tolerant and with a special sweetish volatile smell about him. Kitty's word for this jovial state was *merry*. Then he would sing or romp with the children for half an hour or so of bewildering good humour, before slumping onto the spare bed, snoring loudly, even in the middle of the day. Mummy would be busy elsewhere, Not Noticing.

He was mildly *merry* one teatime when Kitty sidled in from the garden, watchful. 'Put your shorts and shirt on and we'll have a walk,' he said affably. She had a rare sense of being Mr Jones's little girl. Something nice for him to have.

Up the road where on Fridays the Amahs' Market sprang up, its stalls lit at sunset with dangling oil lamps, to sell combs, mirrors, plastic bowls, elastic and thread and needles, cheap sparkly jewellery, poisonous glamorous-coloured sweets and things made of nylon and lace that Kitty took no notice of. Only it wasn't Friday tonight, so the Amahs' Market wasn't there.

Past the Saloon, where men were sitting around tables singing loudly, in a strange greenish light, which Kitty could see and hear through the swinging louvred doors as they passed, with a vague feeling that she wasn't supposed to look, because the men in there were behaving in a way so childish only grown-ups could do it.

Past the market, which was closing now, with its dried fish and curry paste smells, an indescribable aroma which Kitty, decades later, would encounter again, unexpectedly, and say simply, 'Oh! It's *Asia*!'

They stood at last outside the shop where she had been taken for ballet shoes, where a Chinese man with a kind, grave smile had drawn around her bare feet on special paper to be sure the shoes would fit. Mummy never took the children there for ordinary shoes; Bata was in Singapore City, where Kitty didn't wear her old shorts and flip-flops, but her lemon-yellow twist dress with the white bow.

'Which do you like?' asked Mr Jones almost shyly; a surprising conversational opening. Looking in shop windows was fantasy: with Fiona or Brian perhaps, but not with grown-ups.

A truthful child, she confided simply, 'Those are the best,' and pointed to the covetable white sandals, made of only three straps, two across the foot and one around the heel, a pattern of tiny holes forming the shapes of daisies across the toes: cool, dainty, light-hearted little shoes for girls who skip and play jacks without dropping the ball and do country dancing as nicely as they do sums and writing. The height of desirability.

'A pair of those, eh? Like to try them on?'

It wasn't her birthday; she hadn't been especially good. Even if it was, even if she had, she wouldn't have expected this. She believed that her father's cash resources were limitless, but that he rarely chose to expend them. This was a moment of grace and favour as yet unknown. She was too disbelieving to bask in the moment as it deserved.

Cautiously she assented. At the back of her mind was the awareness that Mummy wouldn't like it. But she disregarded it, reckless with the fleeting novelty of choice.

'Come on then.' And they entered the shop.

Kitty wished someone could see her walking home, wearing the perfect shoes – like being barefoot but prettier – and solemnly carrying their box, now empty except for the special tissue paper folded round her old flip-flops.

Back home, Mummy's distaste was as if the beautiful sandals, with their soft and flawless leather, were covered in dog poo or sick. Her mouth changed from a thin scarlet line to a nasty little pursed-up button and her nose seemed to sharpen with scorn. Her eyes were too bright and hard for Kitty to look at.

Daddy's clumsy good humour shrivelled, so she didn't look at him either. His merry-ness shrank back to a little wrinkled withered shoot from the expansive, companionable mood that had prevailed as they strolled together back down Edgware Road. It reminded Kitty of a snail cringing back into its shell from a sharp thorn, pulling in its horns in a rapid, hurt way.

Somehow she had got him into trouble.

'What are you doing wasting money on those nasty common things? She's not going out in cheap rubbish like that.'

'Well, I thought they were all right,' he muttered sheepishly.

'Take them off this instant, Kitty, and put your flip-flops back on. Those are going straight back to the shop.'

'But she's been wearing them.'

'I don't care. Back! Cheap and nasty. Horrible, common things.'

Kitty's hope that Daddy would stick to his guns and override Mummy was fleeting, and soon forgotten. She replaced the sandals in the box, and they weren't mentioned again.

MOTHS DON'T HAVE NESTS

✂

Christine Harrison

'Try it on,' he said in an offhand way.

A moth flew out as he shook it. He held it out, opening up the pale heavy satin lining to view.

At this my heart beat a little faster.

'Has the moth got it?' I sounded as if it didn't matter one way or the other. 'There was a moth. Did you see it fly out?'

'Only one,' he said, then, 'try it on.' He held it out now as if offering an embrace. I slipped myself inside it – it felt different from any coat I had ever worn. Putting on this coat, I was wrapped at once in all the queer bitterness of the past.

'I wonder if there's a moth's nest,' he said, putting his head inside the wardrobe's cavernous space. He folded back the wardrobe door so that I could see myself in its long looking-glass. I fastened the single button of the coat. This fantastically elegant woman in the mirror looked at me.

'Moths don't have nests,' I said rather absently.

The coat was circa nineteen twenty but in perfect nick. Fur

trimmed at neck, cuffs and hem. Voluptuous but not vulgar... I felt unusually ladylike in it.

'Smells sort of spicy in there,' he said. 'Nutmeggy. Not moth balls anyway.'

'Mmm.' I pressed the fur cuff to my nose. 'I really like that smell.' The cloth was the colour of a cut-open nutmeg and with a grain like that too.

'It suits you,' he said. 'You look very posh.'

'Mmm.'

'Will you wear it?' his voice trailed off inside the wardrobe again. 'Books, books, books,' he was saying in a muffled voice. When we bought the house this huge old wardrobe had understandably been left. It wasn't empty.

'Calf bound,' he said smugly. 'Smollet. Gold leaf. Most of the pages still uncut by the look of it. Blast. One volume missing. Blast.' He sat back on his heels looking at his find.

'Possibly. Probably,' I said. 'Yes, of course I'll wear it.' But perhaps I shouldn't wear it that afternoon to visit my friend with her new baby in hospital. If I picked the baby up it might be sick on it.

I would look all right bringing the flowers though. Lilies perhaps would go. Red carnations would look very nice.

'Does Helen like carnations?'

'How the hell should I know.' He had found something else. 'Another book. Russian. Handmade. Just after the revolution I'd say. There was this state-run craft movement.' (Stephen knew about such things). 'Look at these dyes.'

I looked over his shoulder. It was a fairy story book. 'Baba Yaga and the fence made of human bones'. 'The Frog Prince'. He turned the pages with careful fingers.

'I wonder who she is,' he said. We were looking at this beautiful hero girl, fur-hatted and with a coat not unlike the one I was wearing. Underneath it she had on a dress of deepest blood-red. There was a certain look about her of confident savagery, of perhaps ambivalent sexuality, of being part of the natural world and yet having a sophistication that was strange and attractive.

'I don't know who she is,' I said.

We stared at the Russian text which held the answer to the mystery. I felt that I had met her somewhere before. This was no doubt because of the coat I was wearing, in which messages were stitched with invisible stitches. These messages have changed my thoughts.

'Stephen, I must go to the florist,' I said. 'It's nearly visiting time. Will you come?' He was looking through all the little drawers inside the wardrobe and did not answer. 'I'll be off then', I said, as I swept out.

The thing is you can't do that – sweep out – in a modern coat. It would be too lightweight for one thing. A lovely wool and cashmere coat is warm, light as a feather, but has an ephemeral, minimalistic feel. This coat had an erotic weight to it and wearing it I was a different woman.

It wasn't a restricting eroticism, like a corset for example. The coat was loose and easy to wear; I could take long strides in it. I could have done cartwheels in it were I capable of doing cartwheels. At the same time it was heavy and nun-like and hid my body. I loved that.

I picked up the skirt with one hand as I ran down the front steps. Off to the florist to see what red carnations would look like with my coat.

There was a chilly wind. I could have done with gloves as the coat had no pockets. I comforted my cold hands with little strokes of the fur cuffs.

After all I took chrysanthemums to the hospital because of their wintry smell.

'Helen thinks the coat is ravishing,' I told Stephen, 'she wanted it off my back, she said why don't I give it to Christie's to auction.'

'Is that what she said,' his voice was interested but sarcastic as he helped me out of it.

'Or donate it to the costume museum,' I muttered.

I knew I would take no notice of either suggestion. And yet, oh dear, the weight of the past hung on me, it made my shoulders ache. I rubbed them. Please let me have transitory things. China I can smash; things that won't last. Paperback books I can lend to people who won't return them. Actually I've always wanted to live in a tent. And here was Stephen finding more treasures, old cruets and things.

'I shall wear the coat to the concert tonight,' I said. After its years in the dark wardrobe I would take it on an outing that was befitting. In the abbey, listening to Monteverdi, everything would feel perfectly right.

And so it did. Walking up the nave in the interval, I put my arm through Stephen's and he patted my hand. We stopped and spoke to friends. Mary smoothed my fur collar. 'Mink?' she asked in a soft voice.

'She says they've been dead for ages,' said Stephen. 'Anyway I rather like my wife wearing fur.'

I took the coat off.

'Are you too warm, darling? Shall we take a turn outside

before the Finzi?'

I put the coat round my shoulders like a cloak. Cloaks are different. Quite different. Actually it was a cloak the girl in the Russian book had. That was how you could see her blood-red dress. I was that girl – though my frock was not red but green. Not blood-red but forest-green.

I put the coat on properly though, to settle into our uncomfortable wooden pew. As the orchestra tuned up I thought I could catch the faint rustle of those stitched-in messages... I couldn't make out what they were about. Perhaps they were in a foreign language. It was a relief to listen to the Finzi. I withdrew both hands into the furry cuffs and clasped my hands together. It was like having a mink muff.

I sighed and Stephen put his foot against mine. He gets quite bored in concerts if they're playing anything later than eighteenth century.

Anyway I managed to give my attention to the music for a while. But occasionally other thoughts drifted across. It would be best to wear my coat only when going to certain places. Cathedrals. Especially nice tea shops. That sort of thing.

After the concert it was lovely going out of the abbey into the cold starry night and feeling warm, rich and civilised.

But when the cold February weather became even colder and tempted me into wearing the coat to the supermarket my latent snobbery surfaced, making me despise the plastic-wrapped cheese and the mixed bunches of frightful flowers, and, well, practically everything.

'I must buy myself a practical coat,' I told Stephen. 'I haven't got a really warm winter coat – only this one.'

I was unpacking my purchases onto the kitchen table, which

was littered with ornaments, books and pictures – more of Stephen's wardrobe finds.

'If you want to help,' he said, 'put the cat food and baked beans down that end, don't mix it all up. I'm trying to sort out what to keep. What about this thing?'

It was a sampler. They always make my heart sink. I wondered if it had been worked by the owner of the coat when she was a child. 'Susan Butler aged twelve. 1889. Lay not up for yourselves treasures upon earth, where moth and rust doth corrupt.'

'We'll sell it,' I said. 'And I'll take that cruet. And that vase thing.'

'We'll keep the books,' said Stephen.

'I don't think we're going to read Smollet.'

'They'll look good on the shelves. What about the Russian book? We should have it valued.'

'Keep,' I said. I turned the pages to find the girl in the cloak and the red dress. She looked alive, as if about to speak.

'We could learn Russian,' I said.

'*You* can if you like.'

I put the Russian book in the keep pile.

'Look,' I said. 'I'm going into Bath and I'll take the things we don't want.'

'What about the coat?'

'I'm wearing it.'

'It seems to make you cross.'

'Don't be ridiculous,' I said. 'Help me out to the car will you, I can't live with this clutter another minute.'

I took the country road.

Halfway there, after I had driven about five miles I came to a place that always held a frisson for me. I didn't know why. It was moorland fringed with hazel coppice and reeds. It always looked different. In spring there were king cups. Now on this cold still winter's afternoon, the sky was richly coloured as if painted with deep dyes, ochre, cobalt blue and indigo.

I switched on headlights which picked up the eyes of sheep standing by the crossroads sign nearby. I saw a van disappearing in a cloud of smoke down the Bath road.

Then, standing there against the coloured sky I saw a girl. I changed gear and slowed down.

She was just standing there in the desolate landscape. She didn't look lost. She looked as if she owned the place. Owned the world, in fact.

She was tall and had masses of hair, some of it in a wonderful frizz, and some of it plaited into very thin plaits and twisted round her head like a crown or tiara. I slowed right down.

On the ground beside her was a cat in a cage. That settled it, I stopped.

'You okay?'

'Yes, thanks.' She picked up the cat in the cage.

'Going far?'

'I'm okay.'

'Nice cat. Is it for sale?'

She didn't answer but started lacing up her long boots with the string that kept them together, sorting herself out to trek to wherever she thought she was going. I reckoned the driver of the van had left her there suddenly, or she had jumped out, half-dressed, in some sort of rage.

I started the car up.

'Hang on,' she said. I waited while she finished lacing her boots and wound a scarf round her waist. She got in and put the caged kitten on her lap.

'I'm going into Bath,' I said. 'Any good?'

'That's where that sod is going.' She had some sort of accent. Scottish, Glasgow perhaps. 'He'll be round about the abbey square. I'll catch up with him.'

Her anger and the cold air had flushed her cheeks. She had a faint exotic smell – it wasn't patchouli. I was glad as patchouli gives me a headache. The little cat had set up a persistent meowing, showing tiny sharp teeth like little fish bones. She poked her finger in the cage and it chewed her already bitten-raw-looking skin. The backs of her hands were scratched to pieces.

We travelled in silence. She did not seem to want to talk, sitting there eaten up with her inner thoughts. I felt the satin lining of my coat against my ankles as I changed gear and the soft fur on my wrists. I felt more relaxed in my coat beside this ragged muddy woman than at any time I had worn it. She made me feel properly dressed. Was it because she just didn't care or notice, in her outlaw sort of way?

After a while she calmed down a bit.

'I've never seen a cat in a cage before,' I told her.

'Haven't you?' she said, as if there were probably a lot of things I had not seen. I could feel her, from time to time, giving little glances at my coat.

'Nice coat,' she said at last.

'I'm not entirely sure about it,' I said.

'Why's that?'

'Oh I don't know. Feels too much like... I don't know.' How could I explain my ambivalent relationship with a coat?

'I had this great hat once,' she said. 'I lost it at Glastonbury.

It had magpie's feathers in it.'

'Look,' I said. We were coming down into Bath. It looked like a city that had been sacked, smoke rising straight up in the still air to the darkening sky streaked still with thin lines of colour.

'I'll see if there's room in the car park.' Unusually there was plenty of room. It was so cold and there was such a feeling of bad weather to come, everyone must have been at home by their fires. Or perhaps the place *had* been sacked.

As the girl got out of the car she bent over to put the cat cage on the ground while she wound her scarf round her again. Her skirt was fastened with a huge pin at the back and the zip was broken. She appeared to be naked underneath – I had a glimpse of white goose-pimply flesh. I wondered if she had anything at all on under the old skirt and the shrunken Fair Isle jumper with its several moth holes. She stood up and fastened the scarf across her chest and round her waist. Already her hands were blue with cold. A snowflake drifted down from the sky like a message on a piece of paper.

I got out of the car and took off the coat.

'I don't want this,' I said. 'Have it.'

She looked it over carefully as if buying from a dodgy fur trader.

'Try it on anyway,' I said. I felt light. I felt a weight drop from me. I would buy a new coat in Bath that I could take charge of; that would not control me.

She put it on and I knew it was a splendid thing I was doing, giving it to her. The coat revealed what she really was. And I knew it would give her the strength to fight her corner when she caught up with the sod in the abbey square. It would be a weapon for her. It gave her a barbaric swagger. The real animal fur was even part of it. She looked bloody marvellous.

She strode off with the cat, the coat undone, flying out behind her, her wonderful hair and the boots done up with string: the coat going into battle with her.

I knew she wouldn't look after it. She was never going to hang the coat up carefully in a wardrobe. She would probably fling it on the bed at night for extra warmth. The cat would curl up in the mink collar on winter nights. It would start to smell smoky from a wood-burning stove. The moth would eventually get at it. I was glad.

THE GREEN GUERNSEY

✂

Jean Lyon

October

I must live on my own from now on.
Nobody minds what I do any more.
I miss him each day, and the days leak away.
I'm lonely for him, only him.

November

I always tried to live up to Colin's expectations, but never managed very well. When you live with someone, you get into routines and habits that suit you both, and you try to accommodate their expectations and preferences, don't you? He said he didn't mind, but I could see he would have liked a more stylish wife. It would have been good for his image. Not that he didn't love me, you understand. We lived together so long that we explored all the layers of love, even the black holes you fall into when you can't stand the sight of one another. But they were only little holes, and we patched them up well enough.

Like this sweater, in a funny way. He loved this green sweater I'm wearing, with its leather patches. Loden, he called it, this particular shade of green. It's his sweater, of course, but I wear it now because it smells of him. I've worn a lot of his clothes this autumn. His Puffa jacket's nice and warm and the weather's getting colder. Of course I can't wear his trousers or his shoes; they all went to Oxfam or one of those other shops. Kate, my daughter, was very good, you know. Right afterwards, she came to help me sort his things out and she insisted his shoes were the first thing that had to go. She put them in a bin bag and took them away with her, even the new golfing shoes I'd bought for his birthday. She only forgot his wellies and they're much too big for me anyway.

I wear his hats. He had a lot of hats and my head is almost as big as his, so that's okay. His gloves are not a possibility, but I wear his scarves. I also wear his socks. They're too big really. I folded the ends under my foot at first, but it's not very comfortable; I pull them right up now so there's a sort of empty bulge at my ankle.

December

I've decided I'm going to move to a smaller house after Christmas, nearer to Kate. I've started to de-clutter, as she calls it. It's really hard because this house is inhabited by his things, his preferences. It's hard to box up Colin's cricket books. His bat and practice net and balls, they were easy: the club collected them for the boys' team. But nobody wants his books, or his trophies, and certainly not his stone collection. I don't know what to do with his trophies. I don't think they're silver. I must ask Kate what she thinks.

It's been much easier throwing out my own things. My wardrobe was the easiest of all. Wardrobe is a laughable term really, for the things I wear. I kept things because Colin thought I should wear them; fitted dresses, suits, even a pair of shoes with heels, they all went to Oxfam. I've never had a shape that suited fashion. I remember when I wore a miniskirt around my solid hillwalking legs, and summer vests which displayed my chubby arms. I was young then; I copied my friends and thought it mattered.

Then there was a time when I longed for cloaks and gypsy skirts and peasant blouses and shawls. I wore a heavy whirling-dervish skirt once, at a folk festival and it felt wonderful. Colin used to tell people how he rescued me from the hippy life and made me respectable. He was never very clear about how he happened to be at that festival. Every time he told the story at a dinner party, or over drinks, he made up a different fanciful reason. He said he had just been giving a friend a lift, or that he'd been called in to fix the sound system – like, as if! Once he said that he'd been driving by and had seen this girl dressed in red, dancing on her own in the middle of a field and had been irresistibly drawn to her. It was all rubbish really. There were crowds of people there and I've never knowingly worn red, but that's the version I like best.

January

Kate's been here today. She's not very impressed with my de-cluttering. 'Have you read all these books?' she asked and when I said I had, she wanted to know why I thought I'd need to read them again. She's so like her father in some ways. She doesn't approve of me wearing his clothes. She made me promise not to go out in them, you know, to the postbox or the shop. I was wearing one of his cardigans that's far too big and she said I looked ridiculous.

I'm glad she doesn't know that I wear his pyjamas and love the feeling of the cuffs flapping about before you turn them back. There was a film I saw, years ago, with Katharine Hepburn. She was wearing a man's pyjamas and she looked great: feminine and sexy. I'm not really butch, am I? Not if I like to feel feminine like Katharine Hepburn. That's what Kate said. 'Everybody will think you're butch.' Actually she used the word 'dyke'. I really don't like that word. I don't mind 'lesbian'; that's Greek isn't it? Anyway, it's unfair to call people names just because of the clothes they wear.

Colin used to tease me about the clothes I wore. He didn't like me wearing trousers; he said they made me look dumpy. Or sandals. I had to wear the proper stuff for work: a suit or dress and jacket, and tights with everything. How I hated tights. I wore sandals whenever I could, with bare feet, or with socks if it was cold. He didn't like that. He took me to buy some fashion boots once and I was humiliated in the shop: they wouldn't zip up over my calves. I suppose the hillwalking was to blame. I started that when I was at university in North Wales. Colin never took to it. Couldn't see the point of just walking up to the top and then walking down again. But I did get him walking on the golf course once he retired.

I could go hillwalking again, couldn't I? The easier ones

maybe. I might even go on my own. Colin wouldn't let me walk alone, too dangerous. But I've got a mobile phone now and I could let Kate know where I was going. I might even get a dog. No, I can't get a dog if I'm moving house.

February

I asked Kate about all-weather gear for the mountains, like I used to have. She said no, that didn't count as butch, even if I bought walking boots, but did I really want to go walking up mountains at my age? I said yes. I said I planned to do the Snowdon horseshoe on midsummer's day, including an ascent of Crib Goch. I shouldn't tease her, but for a minute she believed me and looked horrified, then concerned. She'd started to put on her social worker look before she realised I was jesting.

That's a nice word. I don't think I've used 'jesting' for a long time. I don't think I have felt like jesting for a long time. Perhaps it's because spring is coming and my crocuses have joined the snowdrops and I have seen the spears of the daffodils poking up through the lawn.

March

I'm not in a hurry to move house, now that spring is here. I think I'll wait until next year. But I'm still de-cluttering. I've got rid of most of my clothes and I've even emptied one entire bookcase, but I can't be expected to get rid of things like the cushions, can I? I do so like fabrics, even though I don't take much notice of clothes. I have always bought remnants, much as Colin bought tools; they'll come in useful some day. This morning I found the silk bedspread I made from the cheap silk shirts that were fashionable in the 80s. I couldn't bear to throw them away at the time, so I cut diamonds from them and made a patchwork of their colours into a bedspread. Colin said it was too heavy (I had to back it with quilting), and we never used it.

It looks lovely on the bed, a bit crumpled, but bright and beautiful. I was sitting on the bed stroking it when I began to cry. About Colin. I have been doing so well. I've been getting on with things. Missing his presence of course, thinking, 'I'll ask Colin what he thinks,' before I remember that I can't. But I'm not giving in. He wouldn't have wanted that either. Kate said so. I still feel guilty though, because he didn't want this damned silk quilt on the bed and I've put it there nonetheless.

April

Kate has been trying to get me to buy some fashionable clothes for the summer. She said the clothes I was wearing when Colin was alive were out of date and I needed a new wardrobe. I've thrown most of them away anyway. All I have now are comfortable, practical clothes. Nothing white, nothing tight, nothing that won't go in the machine. I had a linen dress once, a biscuit colour, and it was wonderfully cool when we were in Greece, but it creased and Colin didn't like that, even on holiday. I ruined it in the machine when we got back.

She said something in navy would be better than the widow's black that I wear. I don't like navy. It's the colour of too many uniforms; nurses, police, schoolchildren. I suppose I just don't like uniforms. What do I like then? I don't think I know.

May

Funny, I always go back to thinking of shawls and saris and bright ethnic clothes that I'd never wear. I like to see them and touch them. But then, as I look around, they are here already. The curtains and cushions and throws are all in beautiful colours, patterned greens and bright blues mostly. They have been here all the time. I chose them and Colin never objected.

I wonder if I could wear greens and bright blues, as well as my black. I had a green corduroy dress once and Colin said he liked it because it matched my eyes. I loved him saying that, even though my eyes are really brown.

June

Kate's not right to expect me to be fashionable. I never have been fashionable from choice. I did as I was told, what was expected. I wore what was expected of me, even when I was a hippy. They were all uniforms, conforming. Now that I can choose I have no idea what I want to wear. I think I'd best stick to practical clothes; I no longer have an image to maintain after all.

I don't often wear Colin's clothes now. Last year I needed to get inside Colin's clothes, to get close to him. It wasn't just for warmth. It wasn't even his smell. They made me feel safe, they protected me, as he had done when I was his wife. I am nobody's wife. I don't know who I am. I used to be someone separate once, so I suppose I have to find out if there's still a separate me.

July

I haven't worn any clothes all day!

It was lovely and warm this morning, and I just walked out of the shower onto the back lawn. It was wonderful to feel the grass under my feet and the sun on my skin. I stood there and lifted my arms up and turned round and round. You could hardly call it whirling, but I started to laugh and I fell on the grass and rolled over and over as if I were a child. I propped myself up on my elbows and my breasts were so small they barely touched the grass. I sat up then and started to look at my body properly. Of course I've looked at my nakedness before, but never in such a happy way, always annoyed that my legs weren't longer, or my breasts weren't bigger or better shaped, and never outside in the sun. A little breeze blew and rippled over my skin. It felt as if Colin was stroking me again. It's a good body; it's served me well, so far. It's never broken down, except when I've had coughs and colds and flu, and it's given me a baby, my lovely Kate.

I put some sandals on and stayed out in the garden, weeding and cutting out last winter's dead wood from the shrubs. I got a few scratches of course, but it felt as if I was part of the garden, part of nature, a native.

Then I heard the postie's van coming down the lane; we live at the end. I rushed indoors and put Colin's dressing gown on, but it was for the sake of the postman, not me. I don't think I would have minded if he'd seen me in my birthday suit. Maybe I would. After he'd gone, I took the dressing gown off, but kept it close by for the rest of the day. I had my lunch outside, and then changed the bed and tidied the kitchen, still without bothering to get dressed. I'm really looking forward to the feel of fresh sheets on my skin when I get into bed tonight.

August

Kate almost caught me undressed today. I told her I had just had a shower, but it was nearly teatime and I had been in the middle of making a cake. She looked at me, but didn't say anything. A bit later she started to ask about what sort of clothes I liked these days. She said she was thinking about my birthday, but that's not until October. I suppose I could get some gardening clothes, jeans and t-shirts that fit. That would keep her happy, and it'll be getting colder by then.

September

I found a bright blue t-shirt with a wolf on it; the ones with dogs on were all pale colours. I've bought myself a Guernsey for the winter as well, in bottle green. I like green, both the colour and the concept. I also got four recycling bins for the back porch. Colin used to say it was a waste of time.

I still don't wear clothes all the time. The house is warm in winter since Colin had central heating put in a few years ago, but it'll be too cold in the garden. I'm not selling the house. I might take lodgers. The other two bedrooms are quite empty now and they're always looking for accommodation for foreign students. Of course that would be the end of my naked days. I'd have to be a respectable landlady. Do I want to take that on? Colin would have hated it, strangers in his house. I don't have to take it on. I can choose. Just as I have chosen the clothes

I need, I can choose how I live. I have begun to step out of the gentle chains that kept me safe. I think they kept me in a uniform though, and I don't like uniforms.

LOUDER THAN WORDS

✂

Hilary Bowers

'Ten…more…minutes,' Zoe gasped, speeding up the treadmill.

'You're pushing yourself too hard, Zoe,' said Rob, her personal trainer.

'But…'

'If you overdo it, you could set yourself back months.'

She nodded. 'Okay.'

'Good girl. Have a shower, go home and rest.'

She grinned. 'No peace for the wicked. I've got a photoshoot at three.'

'Oh, what it is to be young and beautiful. What's the product this time?'

'Some funky new sportswear.'

'You're amazing,' he said softly.

No, driven, she thought but maintained her pose. 'A girl's got to eat, you know.'

'But not too much,' he warned.

'As if,' she retorted.

'See you tomorrow then.'

'Yeh, same time, same place.'

He was still smiling as she left the gym.

After an unseasonable July drenching in the car park, the changing room felt luxuriously warm and Zoe relaxed as an assistant applied make-up after helping her drag on the figure-hugging one-piece running suit.

'Wonderful cheekbones,' the assistant murmured. 'You look just like Audrey Hepburn, apart from…'

'Apart from my hair?'

'Well, it *is* different.'

'Not really, lots of women wear it like this, and it's easier to manage.'

Gel was applied to Zoe's quarter-inch stubble to make it gleam. 'I wish you'd let me put coloured stripes in it.'

'I am *not* a bloody zebra! Don't you think I'm different enough already?'

The assistant's cheeks flushed. 'I'll leave it at that, then.'

'Ready for you now,' an anonymous voice called through the partially open door.

'Thanks,' Zoe replied. 'On my way.'

As she posed, Zoe blossomed. Forgetting everything, she flirted with the cameras and their operators responded; an electrical symbiosis.

Zoe had expected to model one outfit, two at the most, that afternoon but because her name had just been mentioned in connection with the 2012 Olympics the company wanted to jump on her bandwagon; four outfits were to be photographed and she couldn't afford to refuse.

By the fourth change she was exhausted.

Soon be over, she told herself but the cameramen were tired too and the shoot became a stop-start-wait fiasco until Zoe begged, 'Can we stop for a few minutes, my legs are killing me.'

Rageh, the boss, shouted, 'Okay; five minutes, everybody.'

They tried not to watch as she walked over to her chair but they couldn't help themselves, people never could.

Wearily she sat down and took her legs off.

Now no one could bear to look at her; eyes slid away. Devoid of the elegantly curved, futuristic steel prosthetics, she was no longer beautiful, barely even a person. In a world that couldn't tolerate the slightest imperfection, she was an obscenity.

'Can you do a few more, love?' Rageh shouted to Zoe. 'We need more action shots.'

Everyone looked away as she reattached her legs.

But the magic had gone and Rageh quickly called a halt.

If I didn't need the money I'd tell them to sod off, Zoe thought, uncomfortably aware of warning signals from her bladder.

'Need any help?' the make-up assistant asked, hoping for a 'No'.

'Yes, please,' she replied. 'I need the loo, fast.'

After grabbing Zoe's outdoor clothes the frantic assistant propelled her to the disabled toilet where she helped her strip off the stubborn body suit.

'Don't worry,' Zoe growled, 'I can manage from here.'

The cow's actually running away, Zoe noted, hearing rapid footsteps retreating.

*

Her mother and stepfather were just leaving when Zoe arrived home.

'I'll come in for a few minutes, if you need me,' her mother called out as their cars drew parallel and stopped.

'No thanks, I'm fine.'

'Well, this dinner *is* important. Your father—'

'He's *not* my father,' Zoe hissed. 'He's never wanted me around. If Dad hadn't married that bitch I would *never* have lived with you; and I won't for much longer.'

'I've always tried to do my best for you,' her mother whined.

Best, what best? Zoe wanted to scream, remembering the teenage rows. That was why she'd escaped, into the army…

'I appreciate you buying my running legs,' she managed through gritted teeth, biting back the words, *conscience money.* 'And I'm grateful for you letting me use the annexe, but you don't want me here. I'll be gone as soon as my flat is ready.'

'Good. Now, do you mind if we *leave*, Julia?' were the only words her stepfather spoke.

Her electronically-operated bed dominated the lounge, surrounded by stacked, unusable furniture and mounds of clothes. Ignoring the mess, she put some spag bol into the microwave, thinking of her new flat by the canal, and of Chris, coming to visit at the end of his tour in Afghanistan. By then all would be ready.

The advertising job had been a godsend as she'd spent hours, and lots of credit, preparing her new home. You didn't need legs to use a laptop. The wet room was almost complete, doors widened, carpets laid, some furniture already delivered. It was vital that Chris saw her living a normal life. She'd kept details of her injuries to a minimum and sent him carefully selected advertising photos. He must *not* see her as different... diminished.

Eventually she managed to get herself propped up in bed and switched on BBC News 24, anxious, as always, for the latest updates on Britain's battlefronts. Today, once again, Wootton Bassett had turned out en masse to salute the latest casualties – eight coffins – eight more lives lost in less than a week. It could so easily have been—

Her phone rang and her heart leapt as Chris said, 'Hi, gorgeous.'

'Hello, *you*,' she replied. 'You sound so clear...where...?'

'Change of plan, sweetheart. Nobody tells *us* anything. We've just landed. Be with you around six tomorrow evening. You still at your mother's?'

Despite her initial joy Zoe's heart sank. Her stepfather would never allow Chris to stay in the annexe. 'Yes, but it's a bit difficult here. My new flat's almost finished. Let's meet there first then book into a hotel.'

'Can't we stay at the flat?'

Zoe began to panic, she wasn't ready for this. 'There's hardly any furniture—'

'Is there a bed?'

'Two singles—'

'We'll only need one!'

Now she felt sick. I've got to put him off, she thought.

'The bathroom's—'

'Come on, love, we soldiers can cope with anything. Anyone would think you didn't want to see me.'

'Of course I do, Chris, it's just that—'

'That's settled then. I'll bring everything we need. Just give me the address.'

'How long have you got?' she asked after reciting the postcode.

'Ten days, then a training course, you know how it is.'

'Lucky you!' she couldn't help retorting.

'Hang on in there, kid,' he said, voice warm and strong. 'Two more years and I'm out. With your looks and my brains we'll make a fortune. We have a future, gorgeous!'

At last, he'd said it! 'Oh, Chris, I can't wait 'till I see you tomorrow.'

'Me neither, love. Look, I'd better ring off now. See you around six. Bye.'

She turned off the TV and light; no need for medication tonight. Once settled she allowed her mind to drift, recalling the last time they'd made love...

It began as a nightmare but even when she woke, drenched in sweat, the images refused to leave. Flashbacks they were called, but this was no flash, it was her worst experience ever—

Inside the patrol vehicle were her *real* family – mates on high alert, looking out for each other—

The explosion stole away all sound. Centuries passed as she lay dazed, unfeeling, unseeing. Gradually, sound began to infiltrate but humans couldn't cry out like snared rabbits, tortured metal didn't groan—

Something wet warmed her groin. She made the mistake of groping with her hands, and felt something round, hairy—

Her second mistake was to try and see...red...everywhere

red…bodies…bits of bodies…and Taff's head in her lap… nothing else…just his head, one eyeball swinging slowly at the end of a sinewy string, the other, suffused with blood, glaring at her.

Her legs only began to scream later, when medics moved her.

Zoe resorted to sleeping pills and brandy at three and woke feeling half-dead at midday, every movement an effort. Finally she was up, gulping greedily at a mug of coffee.

Her mobile rang as she made toast, excitement giving way to guilt when she saw the number. She hesitated before replying. 'Hi, Rob.'

He sounded concerned. 'You all right?'

'Yes. I'm okay now. Sorry I didn't make it today: rough night.'

'See you tomorrow, then?'

'Er… no. An army buddy's coming to see me. He's arriving tonight.'

'And that will stop you training tomorrow?'

Zoe winced. 'Well, only tomorrow. Lots to catch up on. You know how it is.'

'I didn't,' Rob replied slowly. 'But I think I do now.'

'I'll see you the day after.'

'Right.' His voice was leaden. 'Bye.'

'Oh, *shit*,' Zoe muttered. 'What's got into *him*?' Then she promptly forgot Rob as her eyes swept the room. 'I'm expecting my lover tonight and I've nothing to wear; no slinky outfit, no sexy underwear; oh…shit!'

*

Chris' face lit up when she opened the door and Zoe felt she'd worried needlessly. Bags were dropped and he hugged her so hard she was breathless even before he lifted her up to kiss her. Their mouths remained locked for long seconds before he released her...too suddenly. Artificial limbs are senseless; she stumbled when her 'feet' hit the floor. He frowned as she clutched at him and she shivered as he steadied her, took a step back and fixed his eyes on her face.

'You look fantastic,' he finally pronounced. 'The photos you sent didn't do you justice.' His lopsided smile warmed her. 'And you feel better than ever. Back in a minute.'

'Where's our bedroom?' he asked with a wicked grin when he returned, bags in hand and Zoe felt a spasm of gut-wrenching fear. He was pretending that nothing had changed; well, that was good, wasn't it? She *had* to play along. This is Chris, she reminded herself; my lover, my best friend, my future, I *mustn't* blow it now.

'Down there,' she replied, pointing along a wide passage. 'Second door on the right.'

'And the bathroom?'

'The door at the end, facing you. Did you bring coffee? Would you like some?'

'Yes and yes. Won't be long.'

'Still take it black?' she asked, kettle poised, when he entered the kitchen. Then she took in the pallor of his face and asked anxiously, 'What's the matter, Chris?'

He waved an arm. 'All that.'

She flinched at his anger.

'This isn't *you*, Zoe. The wheelchair, the weird bathroom, that...hoist thing in the bedroom.'

Concentrating on making the coffee she replied, 'From the knees up it's me, Chris and what's inside is still me. The rest is just…well, I've had to adapt.' She gave him her best smile. 'I can do almost everything anyone else can. And some things better. Wait until you see me running!'

He was watching her closely and slowly, his face began to reflect her optimism. 'You're right,' he said, with a decisive nod of his head. 'It was…just a bit of a shock. Sorry, love, I'm an insensitive pig. Look, I'll order some food. Let's forget this and celebrate.'

Zoe smiled again. 'Celebrate what?'

'Us!'

He'd brought champagne. Zoe hadn't officially drunk alcohol since beginning serious training. 'This will go straight to my head,' she laughed, as they tapped plastic tumblers together and, surprisingly, it did. She felt bubblier than the sparkling wine when his arm slid around her shoulders as they sat together on the sofa.

'This is making me hungry,' she giggled.

'Me too, but not for food,' and he nibbled her ear.

Zoe moaned.

'Let's— Oh, bugger,' Chris cursed as the doorbell rang. 'Stay there, don't move,' he ordered as he stood up.

'Yes, *sir*!' she replied, saluting smartly, then she hugged herself, revelling in the sight of him as he strode away, in the sound of him as he spoke to the delivery man then banged around in the kitchen.

'I've put the food in the oven to keep warm,' he said, sliding close to her again. 'I hope you've been doing the same.'

His lips and hands began to work their magic on her body. His gasps and muttered words of adoration reassured her that he still found her desirable as he began to undress her. He was entranced by her high, firm breasts and traced every rib lovingly as he explored further—

He began to unzip her trousers and she realised there was going to be a problem. Chris was breathing heavily as he tugged at the material.

'Not here, Chris,' she whispered. 'It's...a bit difficult. Let's go to bed.'

He looked away as she pushed herself upright and she felt the passion ebbing.' Just give me ten minutes, then come in, okay?' She touched his cheek. 'Okay?'

He met her eyes slowly and nodded. 'Okay.'

She was propped up against pillows and covered to the waist when he came in. She felt his unease, then saw it in his face as he looked down just in time to avoid tripping over her legs.

'Come on...please...it'll be all right,' she whispered, patting the mattress, but he shook his head, swallowing hard.

'I'm still a woman, Chris; look,' and she slowly pushed the duvet down, revealing flat, taut belly, dark, curling triangle—

He groaned and perched on the edge of the mattress, transfixed.

'They're not so bad, really, and you don't have to look...' but in her urgency to convince him she moved, and the severed stumps jerked.

She could hear him vomiting in the bathroom through two closed doors. Stunned into immobility she sat, and waited.

Eventually he knocked quietly on the bedroom door, then,

looking anywhere, everywhere but at her, he picked up his bag...and left.

It took hours before she could bring herself to move, then, stopping only to turn off the oven, she deserted the ruins of her dreams.

Security lay in bed, alcohol and pills. After the second brandy her body dissolved into languorous warmth but her mind was still racing, seeking answers.

Television. Any programme would do. Hercule Poirot? Perfect. The plot didn't matter, the wonderful costumes and sets were sufficiently diverting...until the adverts.

Fascinated, she watched the camera pan lovingly over the contours of a naked young woman. Legs, buttocks, curve of belly, back and arms as the angle changed to hide her breasts, and finally up to her beautiful face. She was flawless, until she smiled, revealing the black gape of a missing tooth.

One missing tooth rendered that gorgeous woman ugly.

She remembered the look of horror on Chris' face, the sound of his retching...and finally understood. She would always be repulsive to others...and therefore to herself.

During the months following the attack, Zoe had cried until she'd run out of tears...or so she'd thought. That night she wept more bitterly than ever, until everything felt swollen to bursting point; tongue, throat, eyes, eyelids, her head...

Even as she cried she posted a message on a website used by other army amputees; a widespread group that had never met but shared gossip, tips, support...but this time the emailed replies she received only made matters worse; at best, tolerance by stoical partners but in most cases, rejection, despite the best of intentions.

*

There was only one solution.

The opportunity to make it meaningful came in the form of an invitation; the means via cautious enquiries and orders on the internet. She kept the curtains closed and only opened the locked door to delivery men.

Her mobile rang many times during the first few days but she refused to answer it and deleted Chris' messages unheard. When he began to text her she switched off her phone, knowing exactly what would happen if they met again. He would be contrite, he would pity her, he would try to…then recoil from her in horror. She couldn't, *wouldn't*, put herself through all that again.

Weeks of mind-numbing solitude were shattered by a frenzied hammering that startled Zoe into stabbing her thumb with a needle.

'Open up!' a male voice demanded. She froze, hoping he'd go away. 'Come on, Zoe, I know you're in there!'

She covered her sewing before unlocking the door.

Rob had never looked like this before; large, looming, angry… but as his eyes swept over her he seemed to deflate.

'At last!' he said. 'Are you all right?'

'Fine,' she replied, staring into his chest.

'No, you're not. Can I come in?'

'Well, I—'

'Thanks. I won't stay long. Just wanted to check you were okay.' He squeezed by her into the squalor of her room then turned on his heel to face her.

'What's going on, Zoe?' he demanded, waving an arm,

indicating the mess: strewn packaging, laptop almost buried by printouts, dressing gown heaped on a coffee table, half-eaten pizzas.

'Nothing.'

'Nothing?' He shook his head. 'Just look at yourself, Zoe.'

'No, *you* look at me! On second thoughts, don't. Look through me, past me but not *at* me. That's what everybody else does.'

Rob blinked. 'Is this anything to do with your friend's visit?'

'Don't…even…ask,' she warned.

'Okay. Sorry.' He held his hands up in submission. 'I'm just here as your trainer, right?'

Zoe shook her head. 'No more training.'

Rob's face blanched. 'Zoe, don't say that, please. Whatever's wrong, we can sort it—'

'*Sort it?*' she screamed. 'How can you sort my fucking legs?'

He held out a hand. She slapped it away.

'I don't want your pity.'

'It's not pity I'm offering,' he replied softly.

'Yes it is. What else is there? You've no bloody idea what it's like, Rob, having to live with these!' Tears ran unchecked down her cheeks. 'I can't be spontaneous about *anything;* walking, peeing, fucking…everything has to be planned.' She began to laugh. 'The choreography of a cripple. Perhaps someone should write a ballet, or a musical: with these feet I could do a bloody good tap dance!'

'Zoe, stop it—'

She wiped her hands over her face and swallowed. 'I have stopped it, Rob. Now go away, please.'

'You've fought so hard—'

'Fought!' she spat. 'And where did *that* get me? You fight illness, sometimes you win but you can't recover from lost limbs, they won't grow back.'

'So you really mean to stop training?'

'Training, modelling, everything. I've had enough. I'm—'

'You're what?'

He's too sharp, she thought, and my tongue's running away. 'I'm...I'm going to do nothing, that's all: nothing.'

'Zoe...'

'No, I don't want to talk any more. I'm tired. Please go.'

Rob walked silently to the door, opened it and turned. 'If you ever need me, Zoe, it doesn't matter what for or when, just call.' Then he was gone.

His parting words saddened her. During the interminable days that followed she often longed to talk to him, to *anyone*, to try and put a stop to the madness but it was Chris who haunted her nights; smiling, tender, lifting her on waves of desire...but always, at the last moment, she would hear the sound of vomiting—

The morning was bright and cold, approaching the 11th hour of the 11th day of the 11th month.

Swathed in a startling scarlet cloak, Zoe was waved, unchecked, through the cordoned-off crowds that surrounded the cenotaph as she wheeled herself, poppy wreath on her knees, up to the police-controlled gap where she was escorted to join the front row of suitably subdued local dignitaries, representatives of the armed forces and veterans. As the brass band played, members of the public pointed, some clapped and cheered, most simply stared at the budding celebrity. The mayor nodded and smiled, the uniforms looked away embarrassed.

Cameras were rolling, local media eager to make much of the young heroine who would lay a wreath in memory of her fallen comrades after the two-minute silence.

The church clock rang out its prelude, the ensuing hush was absolute. Everyone, apart from the media, was so engrossed in their own thoughts that they barely registered Zoe struggling up from her chair before beginning to walk, wreath in one hand, towards the cenotaph steps. The media, sensing a story, did nothing. The two policemen who had just assisted Zoe noticed but hesitated, radioing to see if there had been a last-minute change of plan.

Instead of laying down her wreath Zoe carefully climbed the steps before turning, painfully slowly, to face the crowds and, as her eyes swept over faces only now registering surprise, she faltered; so many innocents…she hadn't realised…if there were only the bigwigs, that bloody pompous Labour MP…she fingered the cloth of her cloak—

Suddenly, shockingly, Chris was there, in his dress uniform, running up the steps towards her. She swooned, knees buckling.

He caught her under the armpits, steadied her.

'Take it off,' he whispered into her ear. 'Disarm it, wrap it in your cloak and give it to me. Make it look casual.'

She tried to move, to look into his face.

'Do it,' he barked. She could feel him shaking. 'Do it for us, Zoe. I love you, I've never stopped loving you. Forgive me, let's try again. We'll make it work. Don't do this to us, to *them*, please.'

She began to struggle with the fastenings, shielded by Chris' bulk.

'How did you *know*?' she demanded of his left ear as he still held her tightly.

'Rob.'

'*Rob*?'

'I'll explain later but he's a good friend…to both of us.'

The crowd gasped when Chris stood to one side, revealing Zoe, starkly beautiful in black body suit, steel legs glinting in the sunlight.

Chris' hand felt warm as he held hers. She squeezed it, whispering, 'I'd changed my mind, I couldn't do it.'

'I'd guessed as much but I had to make sure.'

Their eyes locked.

'What now?' she asked softly.

He grinned. 'You want to make a protest…so make one!'

Zoe's head lifted, her thoughts racing as her eyes swept across the crowds.

'Remember this,' she shouted. 'For every precious British life lost in Afghanistan five more are ruined by injuries like mine.' She paused to swallow and the crowd gaped; silent, expectant.

'Maybe you will remember those who died once a year but we, who survived our injuries, have to battle every day against pain, humiliation and this government's determination to pretend we don't exist.'

The Labour MP began shuffling and glancing furtively around.

'We don't get flown home to pomp and ceremony, we're sneaked in through the back door, scattered in hospitals throughout the country so the media can't discover just how many of us there are. When the government boasts of sending out extra troops, they aren't extras, they're *replacements*.'

At this the crowd began to surge, cheering and swamping the policemen in their eagerness to hear more.

'Hold my waist,' Zoe urged Chris and as he steadied her, she cried, 'This...is for us!' and threw the wreath at the shocked MP. After skimming through the air it hit him on the head, teetering like a bloody crown before dropping at his feet.

During the glorious mayhem that followed, Chris, with cloak and disarmed bomb tucked under one arm, held Zoe firmly as she descended the cenotaph steps. Once on level ground she was in her element and they began to run, hand in hand; not away but towards...life.

IN HER SHOES

Rin Simpson

What do you wear to meet the woman who gave you up more than four decades ago? I'm usually pretty good with clothes – even my daughter Nicky says so, and you know how 14-year-olds are – but today I just don't know. Standing here in the spare room, in front of the double wardrobe Rees bought me when I finally admitted that yes, the one in the bedroom was getting a bit full, it feels like a decision on a par with choosing a mortgage provider.

I love this wardrobe. Armoire, the man in the shop called it. Pompous arse. It's not really French, just a reproduction, but you'd have sworn it was carved by Louis the 16th himself the way this guy was going on. I saw it in the window and just fell in love with its curves and its carvings, the not-quite-white paint that looks like it needs another coat if you don't know it's supposed to be that way.

Beautiful or not, the fact that it's stuffed with so many clothes – skirts and suits and shift dresses and even a pair of dungarees I bought in one mad, pre-menstrual shopping spree and can't bring myself to throw out – isn't helping me to decide what I'm going to wear. And Nicky will be home from school soon. She doesn't know about Claire, about the letter I found in the attic of the woman she thinks was her grandmother. How could I tell her?

Anyway. What about the grey wool suit from Jaeger? I bought that for an interview I think, about a decade ago now, but it's a classic and it still fits. Well, it will with the help of a safety pin. But maybe that's too formal? I know I feel like this coffee we're having is an interview but it isn't, not really. Or at least it shouldn't be.

Rees would probably say jeans. He lives in jeans when he's at home. It's one of the things I love about him, one of many things, the fact that he changes as soon as he gets back from the office, as if to say Mr Jones the shop manager is no more, but I'm here, and I'm all yours. He rarely talks about work once those jeans are on. I suppose my Gap jeans would be okay. They're a bit smarter than the others and I like the way they're not quite bootcut, not quite straight leg. And Rees says they do great things for my bum—

Oh, for crying out loud, I'm not trying to seduce the woman!

But maybe, with a long jumper and sensible shoes? Or those tan boots I got in the sale at Clarks in Cardiff – a real bargain, £120 down to £50, and I got the red patent pumps and a pair of chocolate-brown suede wedges at the same time. It was such a delicious thrill walking home with three bags bouncing against my thigh, none of them for anyone else. And I spent less than £100 too, so I didn't even have to feel guilty.

Thing is though, I'm not really a jeans person. I used to be, when Rees and I got married – I can't believe it's been 20 years – and I do still wear them now and then, when I'm feeling lazy. But I prefer skirts and dresses. They're just a bit more, I don't know; feminine I suppose. I like the way they swish around my knees. Or better yet my ankles. God bless Sienna Miller for bringing back long tiered skirts; they're so useful in the summer when you can't be bothered to shave your legs.

This black and white dress is lovely. I bought it for a friend's wedding last year but decided, in the end, to wear the pink one from Monsoon because Nicky wanted to wear her black and white dress and it would have been far too twee to arrive in mum and daughter outfits. My mum did that to me and I was always mortified. At least…my adopted mum. God, it hurts to think about all that. To have found out now, after she's gone. Never to be able to speak to her about it. I can't decide whether that's a good or a bad thing.

But I don't have time for that now. Back to the wardrobe. Oh yes, the black and white dress. I just don't know.

Hang on a sec, what's that…yes, it is! It's the silk scarf Nicky bought me for Mother's Day last year. Now what's that doing in here? I always keep my scarves in the chest of drawers in the bedroom. The one I lined with wallpaper in a fit of Changing Rooms-inspired madness, when we redecorated after the roof leaked. I bet Rees put it away in one of his cleaning frenzies. He gets those sometimes, bless him, and it's very sweet but I wish he wouldn't. Last time it took me several days to find my kitchen scissors. He'd put them in my sewing box.

Damn, Nicky's home. I forgot she didn't have netball today – something about a PE teacher and a falling out with the head, she said. Not surprised, the head's an intolerable woman. I'd better get the dinner on then. I'll come back to this later. I've still got two days until I meet Claire.

Rees put the light out an hour ago but I feel like someone's been force feeding me Red Bull all day. The meeting…coffee date…whatever, it's tomorrow and I still don't have a clue what to wear.

I asked Rees but he was no use. 'Wear what makes you feel comfortable, love,' he said. Eminently sensible only I don't *know* what would make me comfortable. Not going, that's what. I'm so tempted to email her and call it off. That's all we've done so far, email. Somehow talking by phone would be…cheating. A coward's meeting. No, I have to see her; read her expression as she looks at me, see what she looks like. Whether she looks like me.

I wonder if she'd like that Aran sweater I bought in Mumbles the year Nicky turned ten? I don't know why I remember it was the year she turned ten…oh, yes I do, it was the cake. Ha, that cake; it took me ages to ice. She was very into the sea for some reason, and Dylan Thomas – hence Mumbles – and I decorated it with bilious-looking blue icing and little boats with rice paper sails and even a little plastic dolphin. A gargantuan it would have been to those poor sailors, and half-buried in Victoria sponge: frozen, trying to escape the sugary waves.

Nicky was born in July but that year, the year we spent a week in Mumbles, it turned very cold and very wet all of a sudden, and I didn't have enough clothes with me. 'Pack light' is what my mum – my adopted mum – always said, what I've told Nicky. (She still tries to sneak more shoes into the bag when we go away.) I had one thin cardigan and three pairs of flip-flops, so I went shopping for something warm and found the most enchanting little shop packed with shell necklaces and mobiles made of coral and stormy, passionate paintings of the sea. And this Aran jumper.

But, it's October. Is it really going to be cold enough? I don't need to be greeting the woman who gave birth to me with sweat collecting in my armpits. No doubt I'll be doing enough of that as it is.

Oh, but I forgot that scarf from Nicky. The Mother's Day present. That would be, well, appropriate. And I really love it. 'It goes with your eyes,' she said, before I even got the wrapping off. She'd brought it up on a tray with a cup of tea and a flower from the garden and then stood by the bed, bouncing on the balls of her feet, grinning and waiting for me to haul myself into a sitting position and get my glasses on my nose.

Yes, I think I'll have to wear that. Perhaps with something very simple, like a black pencil skirt and a white blouse. Too much like a secretary? I was one once I suppose, when I left school, before I decided what I wanted to do with my life. Which turned out to be looking after a husband and a house and raising a beautiful daughter. Maybe that's why it's so hard to know that Mum, that Margaret, wasn't really my mum. All the advice she gave me when Nicky was born, the family traditions I thought I was passing down. It's silly to feel like that, I know. She did raise me and she did pass on the things her mother passed to her. Only her mother wasn't really my grandmother.

Perhaps the skirt and blouse are too officey after all. This is a blood relation I'm meeting. Half of my DNA. My physical home for nine months. Oh God, what am I going to wear?

I know, the navy dress. Oops, mustn't wake Rees, he's so tired, poor love. It wasn't an easy day at the shop. He didn't say anything but if after 20 years you can't tell when your husband's worried, you're doing something wrong. The credit crunch isn't making life easy at work. I made shepherd's pie for dinner, and peas and carrots, and leeks in white sauce. Comfort food. He went to bed after the news and I don't think he's moved since.

Such a handsome man still. Not a word that's often used these days, I know – Nicky calls everyone 'fit' and 'lush' – but Rees has always been handsome. A man's man, with a solid frame and strong hands and hazel eyes that almost glow in the right light. He's going grey, more this last year, but he's not thinning yet. And when he sleeps, he tucks his hands beneath his stubbly cheeks and looks for all the world like a 12-year-old. How I do love him.

I'll have to go have a look at that navy dress. I'm not going to get to sleep any time soon and I'll only disturb Rees.

I feel like a teenager on a first date, only worse. If you screw up a first date, at least you'll have a chance to try again with someone else. Oh God, I don't want to go.

I decided on the navy dress after all. It's just a simple shift but it was quite an expensive one, Karen Millen. I got it at the designer outlet centre at Bridgend. If it had been black it would have been a bit too severe, I think, but navy is a good colour on me, or so says the Colour Me Beautiful lady my friend Rachel dragged me to once. And with Nicky's scarf, all swirling turquoise and aquamarine and emerald like the sea, it's a smart, stylish outfit. But, I hope, a friendly one; approachable.

It took me a full hour to decide on shoes. The magazines all say you can wear black and navy together – in fact I saw a pair of patent Mary Janes the other day in Office that were both – but I'm not convinced, same as I'm not convinced pink and orange are good together, no matter what *Grazia* says. And anyway, none of the black shoes I have seemed quite right. There's a satin pair but they're for evening, and a pair of black pumps, and another, sort of squared off at the front with a clumpy heel, which used to be fashionable but seem a bit school mistressy now. I normally wear a pair of plain navy courts with this dress but they're in the shop being reheeled.

In the end, Rees said why didn't I buy a new pair. I just looked at him for a moment, not sure if he was joking, but he laughed and gave me a hug and said, 'Shall I drop you in town?' Honestly, I'm married to an angel. He even came in and helped me look – Nicky's at an ice-skating sleepover thank goodness, or I'd have had to deal with her 'desperate need' for more shoes too.

It was actually Rees who found the ones I bought in the end, in Kurt Geiger. They're not at all the kind of thing I'd pick up: shoe boots with a high stiletto heel and a slight platform at the front, in a sort of soft quilted velvet fabric with patent panelling at the heel and toe, tied up at the front with a wide satin ribbon. There was only one pair left in my size but they fitted perfectly and they're so comfy, even with the stiletto heel.

My legs are feeling a bit shaky now though. We're meeting at a coffee shop, upstairs from a beautiful little interiors boutique I know in Penarth. It's not too big and busy there, I thought we'd have a bit of privacy. Climbing the stairs is a bit of an effort but it's got to be done. One foot in front of the other, it's the only way to go. Too late to back out now.

Oh God, there she is. It must be her; she has the same hair as me. A bit greyer maybe, and a bit shorter, but the same untameable curls. And the cleft in her chin. My dad – my adopted dad – had a cleft in his chin. I always thought that's where I got it from.

She's seen me. I think she's said my name, I saw her lips moving, but there's a rushing sound in my ears. I feel a bit sick.

She's getting up, stepping out from behind the small wicker table. She's wearing navy shoes. Stiletto-heeled. Quilted velvet. Tied with a ribbon.

I look into her eyes. The same blue as mine. I smile, and walk over to where she is waiting.

WELL TURNED OUT

✂

Sue Coffey

That's funny. She's usually got the kettle on by the time I get here. Hope she isn't sulking because Liam was rude when he took the call. He's always riled by her 'Lady of the Manor' voice. It's to do with the fact he doesn't like his mum going out cleaning. It's hard for him to understand that though I don't need to do it these days I'm used to it. Harriet only meant well, ringing up to warn me she wanted the loft sorted out. Liam relayed an exaggerated version of the message: '"Of course, it's impossible for *me* to clamber up there after the hysterectomy. But Di will need to be careful too. That ladder can be precarious whether one has a womb or not—"'

Right, coat off. I must get a new one. Liam grew out of this when he was in the comp and he finished university two years ago. It's got my shape now, even when I'm not in it; bent at the elbow, bulging bum. Hanging there over Harriet's Gallic gardening smock it looks like the odd-job man giving the French maid a bunk-up. Reminds me of the barbecue when the mongrel gatecrashed and gave their precious Schnauzer a good seeing to. All that yelping: mostly from Harriet. 'Do something, Rowland!' Him running up full tilt with the hose, when it jammed he went arse over tip into the pampas grass. Laugh! I nearly dropped my tray. Poor bitch wandered off and got run down next day. That's proper sex. Leaves you so dazed you'd not noticed being hit by a double-decker. If memory serves.

Can't think where Harriet is. Oh well, two minutes peace for a change. She's left out the dressing-up bag for me I see. The state on these slippers – spreading in all directions, sorry-for-themselves heels. They look the way I feel. I used to dream about wearing a uniform when I was a kid. Saw myself as an air hostess or a nurse. This get up is a bit different: peasant footwear and an old cake shop overall. There. Let's have a twirl. Wond-er Wom-an! Huh, Skiv-vy Wom-an, more like.

Never mind. A spot of posh instant will soon set me up. I hope Rowland isn't around today. Creep. I marked his card even before I met him. The advert said it all: *Willing young female of good character wanted for household tasks.* What century did he think we lived in? The interview confirmed what I suspected. You could see him thinking, 'Older than I'd have liked but a distinct possibility.' While Harriet asked sensible questions he was busy flirting. 'Ah, Diana! Named after the goddess?'

'No,' I said, doing my best to look 'saucy'. 'After Diana Dors, my dad was mad about her.' Well, I was desperate for the job. And it did the trick.

I always call *him* Mr Willoughby-Jones though it was 'Harriet' practically from the off with her. I've heard him take issue: 'She's your cleaner, darling, not your friend.' Even though he doesn't like me any more he still ogles. These bleach splashes don't help. X marks the spot. They make me look like a nymph in one of those paintings: starkers except for a strategic wisp of gossamer. They'd be amazed to think I go to galleries and museums regular. Bet they think the only thing I pore over on my days off is a bingo card.

Mmm…that's good. Expensive coffee gives you more somehow. It's the same with Rowland's aftershave, that fancy Marks and Sparks potpourri or the new leather tang in their car: the comforting smell of money. Well, who am I to knock it? If it wasn't for what Rowland gave me—

Ah, here she comes, tripping down the stairs, all done up like a dog's dinner to sit in the conservatory all morning and chat on the phone. I wish I could tell her that all the advantages of quality skincare can't turn Mrs Mutton into Miss Lamb, and that long, platinum blonde hair doesn't help turn the clock back. We were born the same year, not that she'd ever admit it.

It's time for me to get my face ready too. The one that says: 'What's first? I simply can't wait to start buffin' and polishin'.'

Look at it. You can't move up here. The only thing in my attic is that suitcase of Gary's belongings. I should chuck it. I mean, fifteen years. Stupid to think that there might still be a letter, a knock on the door.

All these paintings of nudes. Better up here in the dark than down below, I suppose. Rowland's taste, obviously, like this one – Rubenesque – is that a word? Big girl sitting there with her spine twisted like a barley sugar, peeking over one shoulder. The size on those buttocks! They'd weigh more than Kate Moss and Naomi Campbell put together. I'd have refused to do that pose; I can feel the crick in her neck from here. They're not even much good, anyone can see that. Except for Rowland. I can just imagine him flashing his cash. Art bought on the basis of nipple and crotch for his pound.

It didn't seem odd after the first time, slipping off the kimono and taking up my position. I expected to be embarrassed, hear people sniggering, but there was none of that. I felt…beautiful, being *considered* by the students. When I undressed at night it was to get into bed by myself and I missed my appreciative audience of one. Stripped down I felt more equal to others than when I was wearing my tired old clothes. Course, my body was still in good nick seven years ago. And even if I did end up getting laid on the *chaise longue* at the end of term it was every bit as much my idea as 'Sir's.

He was a nice man. If Liam hadn't been going off the rails at the time it might have gone somewhere. Not that I gave the poor bloke a chance to get involved in my problems. Everything was so difficult. Half frozen: money, life, my son, me—

The evening classes I go to now aren't much cop. We just practise cross-hatching with stubs of pencils on sugar paper. It's like being in Top Juniors. It gave me quite a turn to see his face in that prospectus yesterday. Lifelong Learning Art History course at the university: sounds interesting. Wonder if it's booked up? The blurb said that he's been living away for years. That'd explain why I never did bump into him in the museum or art gallery.

Right, that's this side done. I'll tackle the big chest next.

Whew! I'm sweating like a dray horse. Those curtains and rugs weighed a ton. Still, it beats fannying around with a duster.

One false move and a single figurine could cost me weeks of wages. Not that Harriet would charge me. But I don't want any favours. I've got my pride and can't bear people feeling sorry for me just because Gary...what? Died; ran off with another woman; lost his memory; emigrated? Take your pick. I wish I could. Settle on one theory, I mean, and stop driving myself mad. Chances are I'll never know what happened, though I've re-lived that morning 'til it's threadbare.

Gary: eating toast. Me: washing up, singing along to the radio. He picked up his keys. I turned from the sink and said we should decorate Liam's bedroom for his eighth birthday. He said: 'Team colours.' I said no. Blues and greens I wanted, like the ocean. Liam loved dolphins. I'd paint a mural. He said: 'The DIY shop's got a sale. We could go down tonight.' I said okay. He said: 'See you, Babe.' I didn't look round. Didn't kiss him. I heard the van pull off. They found the van.

What do you tell a kid who keeps asking where his dad is and when he's coming home? They were so close those two – football, fishing. I tried everything: hospitals, police, Salvation Army. But the special days kept coming and going with no word – birthdays, anniversaries, Christmases. It's true what they say about old habits dying hard; I catch myself, sometimes, staring out of bus windows at passers-by.

Now there's Liam's wedding and he won't say what he's thinking outright. But he dropped it into the conversation the other day: 'I reckon we'll get a good turn out at the church.' And there was something in his voice. He hasn't given up hope. Part of him thinks there's still a chance his dad will be there. In a pew, smiling. Oh, shit! What am I crying for?

Talking of daft dreams: why has Harriet collected all this

baby paraphernalia? If she conceived now she'd baffle medical science. Poor thing, perhaps that's the reason she pretends: turns a blind eye to all his carrying-on. She said to me once, 'Children just didn't happen for us – no one's fault.' But it was Rowland's voice I could hear, making her feel guilty and a failure for denying him a son. Not that I can imagine him being prepared to share star billing with anyone – let alone her money.

Nice frame on this mirror; pity about the picture currently showing. If 'Sir' were here he'd wonder what he ever saw in me. He used to say back then that my dark, wavy hair put him in mind of Janey Morris. Course, he had to explain who she was, when she was at home, and a lot more about the Pre-Raphaelites besides. It wasn't your average chat-up line. I wish I'd trusted him when I had the chance. But there'd been too many men saying whatever they thought would get them into my knickers. I should have followed my instincts instead of backing off. He wasn't like Rowland – it was never a case of anything with a pulse. I wonder whose assets his Lordship was juggling last night. Conference, my arse…or not, thank God! I bet Harriet doesn't know about all these smutty books hidden under the Folio Society collection.

It was hanging around college got me into the printed word. And reading up on grants and bursaries saved Liam.

Now look at him: professional job, promotion in the offing, getting married. I can stop worrying, or, as he never tires of telling me, using him as an excuse for not doing more with my life. Thing is, once you're in a rut it's hard to imagine any other way. Where would I start? I suppose I could always follow Harriet's example. Take up hobbies and socialise, flower arranging one day, T'ai Chi the next, 'do lunch'. I could smuggle some of this stuff out under my coat: tapestry, tennis, mandolin. When all that palls I could plan a series of parties with elaborate themes.

That New Year's Eve 'Arabian Nights' one was entertaining enough, one way and another: yashmaks, turbans and jewelled sandals everywhere. They were in their element. Rowland enjoying all the flesh on display, stuffing notes into the belly-dancer's costume and Harriet rushing about in aquamarine chiffon, showing off her enhanced attractions and saying it was 'the best yet' and 'such tremendous fun'. Rowland made a speech calling her his 'golden-haired Scheherazade' and toasted 'the wind beneath my wings'. Harriet swallowed it all. I wanted to throw up.

Come midnight I had to be by myself. 'Should auld acquaintance be forgot' always gets to me. I thought it was strange that the light was out down in the basement, or 'wine cellar', as Rowland likes to call it. Then I heard him whispering 'Happy New Year' close by. Gave me a hell of a fright. I found the light switch a bit sharp and there they were: a pair of rabbits caught in the headlights. Him with his trousers down while one of his 'secretaries' treated him to a touch of Eastern promise. I gave him an old-fashioned look. Couldn't help myself. Harriet doesn't deserve it – least of all in her own home. As for him, he was mad that he'd been sussed and by the domestic, too. Although the secretary's jealous partner had a pretty good idea of what was going on. I wish he'd carried out his threat to give Rowland a cold shower. He wouldn't have needed the water feature that was mentioned either. Not with a perfectly good flush toilet in the cloakroom.

All these designer suitcases stuffed full of clothes. Lots of her things have still got the price tags on. And they're so small. Harriet's obsessed with maintaining her BMI, whatever that is. She'll be blending celery and crispbreads next. If she gets any thinner she'll fade away completely. I could save her time by telling her how to achieve invisibility.

The trouble is, when you *want* to re-join the world it's terrifying. I've been putting off getting an outfit for this wedding for months. Time's running out but just the thought of fitting rooms brings me out in a cold sweat. Harriet dresses as if she's twenty-one and I've got the wardrobe of a bag lady. Which of us is the bigger fool?

Whenever I'm getting ready to leave I think of Rowland coming to look for me at the end of that party, after Harriet had gone to bed. I thought I was looking at the sack but he was on another tack entirely. Said he wouldn't be blackmailed. Like I'd go in for anything like that! He was blustering but you could see he was scared stiff that the goose that lays the golden eggs would fly away. As if she'd have believed me. I told him where to stick his cheque but he just got furious and shoved it in my hand. He said that if I tried to get more he'd fix it so I wouldn't work round here again. I was stunned. It might have been a drop in the ocean to him—

Ah, here's Harriet. I'll get my face ready, the one that says: 'Same time next week?' And then I'll hand in my notice. I'm not going to have time for other people's mess. Not when I need to put my own house in order.

I am Wearing no Make-up

✂

Kerry Steed

When I first meet you I am wearing no make-up.

I am wearing no make-up. My hair needs washing, my clothes too. I am exhausted. If I were a tortoise I would take all of myself into the dark shell of my own space. I would float into the darkness; stare into it and attempt the art of not thinking about anything.

I am not a tortoise. I have no shell.

I am homeless. And I don't even have a cardboard box.

I am living out of the boot of my car and on the goodwill of friends who have floors.

When I first meet you I am wearing no make-up. I am exhausted. I am living in a conscious dream. I could believe that you don't exist.

I have borrowed a friend's bath. It is mine for all the time that the water is hot enough. I lie in it and stare at the ceiling.

My friend has two goldfish in a tank on a cabinet next to the bath, and sometimes I stare at these instead of at the ceiling. As they glide around their home they have lots of time to talk to me, silently, opening and shutting their mouths. Occasionally I humour them by talking back in the same way.

They are lucky these goldfish, they have a home and no need to think about where they are going to sleep tonight or tomorrow night. They have no worries about when and where to do their laundry. They don't wear clothes. They don't have to think about what to wear.

They don't even have to put on make-up; they are already golden and shiny.

Lucky bastards.

I normally wear clean clothes. I normally wear make-up. Not a lot but enough to make me feel shinier than I might be feeling inside.

Sometimes an unexpected situation can break habits that you have developed over years.

I am not normally homeless. I don't normally take baths in other people's bathrooms and examine cracks in other people's bathroom ceilings.

I am tired; I am lying in a bath that is not my own. When I have finished, I will not go to a wardrobe and take out the clean clothes that I have decided to put on to see my friend. I will not stand in front of the mirror that I look into every day and put on make-up.

Sometimes an unexpected situation can take what you have come to rely on as your normal self by surprise.

Instead, I put on the same clothes that I wore before I got into the bath and I rub the steam away from a mirror that is a stranger to me. I gather up my hair on top of my head and clip it there to hide the fact that I should have bothered to wash it. I examine the spot on the side of my chin. I acknowledge that make-up would make me shinier. I acknowledge that I am too tired to act on this.

I am having dinner with one of the few friends who I will allow to see my bare face, even if it resembles a pizza. This makes me wonder why I bother putting on make-up for people I don't know. Shouldn't it be the other way round? Shouldn't I want to look my best for the people I love the best? But wearing make-up doesn't make me a better friend, or even a better person.

I am too tired to try and work out the paradox I have just presented myself with.

I do not put on my coat, walk out of my own front door and close it behind me. I have no front door to walk out of.

The funny thing is that if I weren't homeless then maybe I wouldn't be going to eat with my friend at all. Normally I can cook in my own kitchen.

I wouldn't be meeting you at all, if I weren't homeless.

So what does it matter about the clothes and the make-up?

I swirl the bath out with clean water. I hope that I have left the bathroom as I found it. I nod to the goldfish. I go downstairs. I wish that I could find nothing there but silence: when you have nowhere to live you long for the silence of your own shell.

I walk across floorboards to a glass door. Through the glass I see the back of a stranger, sitting on a step that leads down to my friend's kitchen.

I am wearing no make-up. My hair needs washing, my clothes too. I am exhausted. If I were a tortoise…but I am not.

Silently I push open the door.

And there is the stranger, sitting talking to my friend: my friend with whom I wanted to be silent.

There is the stranger: to whom, it seems, I will have to talk.

I have a spot on my chin and am exhausted, so much so that I want to cry.

I wish my friend had warned me about the stranger. I would have made myself feel shinier. I would have visited the launderette. Am I dreaming up the stranger to torment myself because cracks have appeared in what is normal?

I step forward; they keep talking. They haven't got wind of me yet.

I step forward and a floorboard creaks and the stranger turns around and all I can think is: 'I am wearing no make-up, my hair needs washing and my clothes too.'

You turn around and you are looking at this dirty-clothed, barefaced version of me and I feel...I feel that I wish I had made myself look more human.

I don't want you to be there, I don't want you to be looking at me but you are. I don't want to be feeling what I am feeling, thinking what I am thinking, because it makes me feel vacuous.

Have I nothing to feel and nothing to think about you, you who I am meeting for the first time, because all I can worry about is how I look? Are you worried? Do you care about the spot on my chin, the stain on my jeans? Why would you, you don't even know me.

I have never made up my mind about first impressions. Do they count for anything or not? And why am I worrying more about the first impression I am giving rather than the first impression you are?

At what point in my life did it become so normal to wear make-up and clean clothes that I feel uncomfortable if I don't? When did my appearance come to mean more to me than meeting a friend of a very dear friend?

I am questioning myself so much that I lose the chance of saving my first impression of you. My friend must say something, you must say something, I must say something, but anything anyone says dissolves into my own thoughts and becomes unsaid again. Until:

'I am going to go and look at your fish,' you say to our friend.

The two fish in the tank are a recent acquisition.

'Yes, do,' says our friend. 'They're good to look at. It's therapeutic.'

You disappear to look at the fish. I am glad; they are shiny enough and won't mind you looking at them.

I catch sight of a vague reflection of me in the glass of a picture frame. I automatically feel for the spot on my chin.

'Don't pick,' admonishes my friend.

I put my hand into the pocket of my jeans.

'I'm glad you're here tonight,' she says. 'It's good that you two could meet.'

I sit down on a chair and examine the picture in the frame. It is easier to do so now that my reflection is no longer mixed up with it.

'We're going to the pub later, want to come?'

I blanch; I am wearing no makeup, my hair needs washing.

'Where are you sleeping tonight? You're welcome here.'

'Thank you. I've a sleeping bag in my car.'

Going to the pub with no make-up on is the price to pay for a bed that night.

When you return I wonder if the fish enjoyed looking at you. You do not wear make-up. Like them, you do not need to. Your skin is unblemished and your features strong and beautiful.

It is enjoyable, looking at you.

It is more enjoyable looking at you than thinking about the spot on the side of my chin. As I look at you, the spot, which had been the largest continent on the globe of my face, starts to shrink.

You are wearing no make-up. And you tell me that your washing machine is not yet plumbed in and you are running out of clean clothes.

You tell me that you think my top is nice.

'Which one, my green knitted cardigan or my top underneath it?'

'Both,' you say and pull at my cardigan and smile.

You are enjoyable. You are enjoyable and you are kind and you have just made me feel better. The thought that I am wearing no make-up is becoming acceptable.

'So, coming to the pub?' you ask.

I smile.

I am wearing no make-up. My hair needs washing and my clothes too. I am exhausted.

If I were a tortoise I would stick out my neck and my head so that I could enjoy being with you.

I look at you. I look at you wearing no make-up. I look at your knitted jumper that needs washing. I look at you and you look beautiful.

I smile.

'I like your jumper. And yes, I'm coming to the pub.'

Going to the pub with no make-up on? It no longer seems like a price to pay for a bed for the night.

When I meet you again I am still not wearing make-up.

I am not wearing make-up but I am another day nearer to having my own front door. I have visited the launderette and I know where I am going to be sleeping that night.

Later we lie tangled up together and you start to cry.

'You okay?'

You smile and nod and delicately wipe away your tears with a finger.

'Sure you're okay?'

You nod again, smile again.

'Just happy, though I wish I weren't wearing mascara.'

'Why are you?' I ask.

You don't reply, but you don't need to. I know why you are wearing mascara.

'You don't need to wear make-up,' I tell you. 'You are beautiful.'

I draw you closer and carefully wipe your tears away myself. You have cried the mascara from your eyes and now we are both not wearing make-up.

I like knowing that you are happy. I like knowing that you wanted to show me you at your best. But you are your best because you are *you*, not because you are wearing mascara.

We meet a third time, a fourth and then more and more times until we lose count and it's not like meeting at all but just being together; and sometimes we are wearing make-up and sometimes we are not. Sometimes my hair is clean and your clothes are dirty and sometimes it's the other way around. But all the time I feel that I am more honestly myself with you than I have ever been with anyone else. And I feel that you feel that way about yourself too.

When we first met we weren't wearing any make-up. We were both running out of clean clothes.

A barefaced first meeting: there was no peeling away of layers to get to know each other.

Sometimes an unexpected situation can break habits that you have developed over years. Sometimes it can take what you have come to rely on as your normal self by surprise.

And sometimes, it can bring you unexpected happiness.

A Handbag to Die For

✂

Stephanie Tillotson

It's embarrassing. Really embarrassing. I have no idea how I got here, to this long, wide and open, empty beach. I opened my eyes and, at first, thought I'd fallen asleep at a barbeque or a beach party. I've looked up and down the shoreline and I can't find anyone – no one at all. I don't have a hangover and there are no signs of a fire: no cans, cigarette butts, in fact no litter at all, nothing to show that any human being has been here recently – if ever. That's a relief in a way, because if there were crowds of people, this would possibly be my worst nightmare. When I woke up, just a little while ago, the first thing I realised was that I was dripping wet. The next, that I was completely naked.

It must be some sort of joke – someone will turn up soon with a towel and tales of what a laugh it has all been. Maybe we came out here skinny-dipping and this is their way of getting back at me because I wouldn't go into the sea. But who would leave me out here like this? Alistair wouldn't do this. For one thing he wouldn't think it funny – stupid and immature yes, but definitely not funny. His face when I bought him a strippergram for his 40th! He seemed to think we were laughing at him because he 'married beneath him', as he so pompously put it. So maybe he's trying to teach me a lesson, though I can't remember what for. Still, I'm sure that he will come and get me before long. Really, there's no reason to be anxious; I just need to take a few deep breaths and wait.

It's a beautiful, still evening; the sky is black with a million tiny, hard stars shining. I feel I could understand infinity looking into that darkness tonight. The moon hangs heavy, full and bright, reminding me of the shiny ten pence pieces my mum used to save for me to put in my school purse when I was a child. Everything looks very clear, so sharp that I can see the crater rings burnt into the moon. Though the colour of crude oil, the sea is calm, and there is nothing to hear but the waves gently breaking. I could be in paradise if the sand were golden and soft, but it isn't, it's dark and slightly gritty. That's why I am walking through the shallow water, so that the gravel is washed from my bare feet. And it is warm, which is good, given my situation. Despite the heat I am so wet my hair is plastered flat against my head. Now that is odd, as I can't have been in the sea because, though I love beach holidays, I hate the sea.

Something else is strange. Despite it being night there ought to be a sound, a car, a plane, something. We are too close to the city for it to be this quiet. Even the gulls must be asleep. Now I remember waking up on the sand and being aware that I was lying in the middle of a deep silence. But there's another memory, one of folding my clothes up and putting them in a neat little pile with my shoes in a pair, side by side. Perhaps I left my clothes and shoes somewhere on this beach. Where is my handbag?

Ah, yes, the leather handbag – that's why Ali was so very angry.

What was that? Listen! Stand still and listen. There it is again – an awful noise. It sounds like a child crying. Perhaps it was a fox. I remember the first time I heard a fox's mating cry I had to wake Ali up because I thought someone was being murdered at the bottom of the garden. He laughed at me and said I knew nothing. But I've lived in the city all my life. There, that terrible cry again. I think it's coming from behind the rocks at the cliff wall. I'll peep round quietly and try not to frighten the creature—

Dear God, it is a child! A little boy, a lost boy of about eight or nine, his tiny legs have grown long and skinny, his chest so thin I can see his ribs. He's clinging on to an azure-blue lilo bed that has a crude picture printed across it, an octopus in the shape of a smiling bubble, waving its plastic tentacles everywhere.

'Hello,' I say, worried in case I frighten him. He stares at me, just stares, hard, out of big, round, beautiful blue eyes. He has blond hair with a long fringe that keeps falling in his face so that he has to shake it out of the way and he's been swimming because he's wearing little trunks and his hair is wet through, as wet as mine. 'Are you all right, poppet?' I ask him and the child's mouth falls open. 'What are you doing out here on your own? Is there anyone with you?'

'I'm looking for my daddy,' the boy answers. 'I can't find him anywhere, though I've called and called and called.' Then he begins to cry again, a terrible noise, a horrible wailing sound in his chest as if he is choking on his own sobs.

'Never mind,' I say, trying to distract him, 'we'll find your daddy, don't you worry. What's your name? '

The child's sobs have become a gurgling, low reverberating moan rumbling through his little body, and I can feel myself starting to panic again. 'You can call me Helen,' I suggest.

'Helen,' he cries, reaching out towards me, his fingers white, wet and twisting up into the air. Then he makes a sound as if he is going to chuck up and I move back a step or two just in case when, with a loud retching noise, he opens his mouth and out comes a stream of green-grey water that smells strongly of salt and dead fish. Suddenly the boy's head does this funny, twitchy sort of thing and he starts screaming. I stumble away from him but I can still hear him gushing up the water and crying, 'Daddy, Daddy, where are you? I'm scared here all on my own.'

So am I, I think, sitting down behind the biggest, blackest boulder I can find and wrapping my arms around my bare legs. I can feel myself rocking backwards and forwards I am so afraid. Tears begin to run down my face, as if the humid air has suddenly broken and I am caught in the centre of the storm. I close my eyes and cover my ears with my hands to shut out the long, wide expanse of beach and the pitiful crying of the child.

It's dark. Pitch black, not even the stars are shining, cold and hard. I can smell the faint scent of roses, a sweet and cloying perfume. Water is lapping at my hairline, warm water hugging me. It is so quiet, and then I hear the soft knocking of knuckle on wood, gentle but insistent, somewhere close to my left ear.

'What do you want?' I demand.

Ali's voice answers, 'Please let me in.' He sounds contrite, sad. 'I'm sorry about everything,' he says, 'please, let me in. I'll make it up to you.'

'Go away.' It is my voice, I sound shocked, as though I have been crying recently. Ali's loud footsteps thud away. He is angry again.

I opened my eyes and I was in my bathroom at home. The blind was still up at the window pane and outside the night was black. I was lying in the bath and rose petals were floating across the surface of the warm water. The chrome taps were misted with steam and the cream tiles running with condensation. Everything here is my choice, clean, modern, expensive, but, as Ali said, I spend more time in the bathroom than he does. I love lying in the bath, choosing from the arrangements of bottles tinted with oils and moisturisers, creams and gels. Tonight I plan to use my latest acquisition, an unguent that smells faintly of lemons, of luxury, of exotic southern Spanish holidays, all held in a clean white pot that only cost me £30. I can see my clothes where I have left them tidily in a neat pile, my shoes together as a pair, side by side.

Ali had gone beserk. Absolutely ape! And all because of that handbag. It seems that he had started going through my things, my wardrobe, my papers, my bags, my pockets. I don't know what he was looking for, but he found it: a receipt for an expensive, designer leather handbag. When I got home that night he was so angry. He shouted at me, he shook me until I could feel my neck bruise and stiffen. He threw plates, knives, turned the tables over, cleared the kitchen tops with one sweep of his arm and deliberately broke a window with my ivory statue from South Africa. Somehow he broke that too. He'd thrown things before, even at me, but never, never his fists. So I had locked myself in the bathroom. After he'd banged on the door and screamed at me for over an hour he eventually went away and I heard the front door crash to behind him. Suddenly the house was quiet and still.

I ran a hot bath and dropped in my last scented fizzer; the ones that dissolve and leave a bed of rose petals floating across the surface of the water. I was so tired, so achingly tired that I closed my eyes and I must have fallen asleep because suddenly he was back, tapping on the bathroom door again.

'What?' I sighed, looking down at my body lying in the water, my finger ends white and matted.

'I'm worried about you, darling,' he said softly. 'You've got to wake up. You can't fall asleep in there. It's not safe; people accidentally drown falling asleep in the bath.'

'Go away, Ali.' I replied 'I just want to be on my own for a while.'

'Please, Helen,' now he was begging. 'Please let me in. Why don't you love me anymore?'

Tears spilled and ran down my face, sliding over my shoulders and into the warm water. Nobody believes me when I say I love my husband. Because I do. They think I married him for his money. People think that, I know they do. They think I use him and perhaps I have been guilty in the past but he wanted to look after me and I let him. I know he wishes he could have the girl back, the girl I was when first I met him. The one who was full of hope, the one that, now I know, Alistair thought he could mould into whatever shape he wished. But though I didn't want to be morphed, I loved being his wife. I loved the way he rested his arm across the back of my waist whilst he talked to his friends. I loved sitting next to him when he drove, his powerful, supple hands working the steering wheel. I loved my life; I thought I was the luckiest bitch on the goddamn planet. But I didn't love the way he left me and it was a big house to be alone in. He stopped coming home until late at night, when he was full of noise and whisky. So I decided I would try and win him back. I decided to go shopping.

Some women would have found a priest to talk to, some taken a lover or two, others would have indulged in drink or food – some given up eating altogether. I could have found a hobby or a charity to support or discovered bad health but instead I spent money. To begin with I thought I was doing it for Ali; slippery satin nightclothes in purples and pinks, then underwear, silk and lace that Ali adored. I was encouraged. I bought elegant coats, knee-length leather boots, beautiful hats, vertiginously high-heeled shoes, long evening dresses with open backs and exposed shoulders, necklaces, earrings and tiny, sequinned evening bags. Then I discovered I was doing it for me – spending had become my secret and greatest pleasure. I loved being drawn into the sensuous surroundings of expensive boutiques, wrapped in attention, colour, contour, cloth, fussed over and petted, seduced by the invitation to try it on in the back room, scented and cubicled with heavy velvet and brocade curtains. I loved the endless possibilities of the high street shops and department stores, and above all I loved being the centre of attention, even if I had to pay for it. I was like a child I suppose, but at least I felt alive. I was seen, if only by a mirror in a changing room. I wasn't a ghost wandering around an empty house. I tried every diet published and as I grew thinner the credit card bill gained more and more weight.

He was still tapping, slowly, gently but insistently knocking on the bathroom door.

'Oh for God's sake, Ali, stop that!' I shouted.

'I just want to say I'm sorry, please let me in.' He knew that pathetic, whining tone would make me angry enough to open the door. I reached out and turned the key in the lock. The door flew open with a crash and Ali stumbled in, tripping over my tidy stack of clothes, my shoes neatly together as a pair, side by side. Turning to me, he caught his foot in the strap of my expensive, designer leather handbag, the one that had caused all the shouting. I know £900 is a lot of money, I'm not stupid. But I had seen it and just had to have it, you know how it is. I thought 'that handbag is just to die for!' It wasn't my fault he found the receipt. If he hadn't gone looking through my pockets—

'Watch out,' I snapped, 'That cost me a bloody fortune.'

Tearing at the strap around his ankle he ripped the soft leather in two. I could hear myself screaming with rage. I slapped the surface of the water so that it splashed Ali hard in the face, lapped over the edge of the bath and soaked his trousers and bare feet. Suddenly he held me by the neck with one hand, pushing me back against the bathroom wall, covering my mouth with his other hand.

'Bitch,' he hissed, through clenched teeth. 'It's time someone taught you a lesson'. His eyes were hard and angry and I wondered if it were true, what he was saying. That I had come to love my clothes more than I loved my husband. I fought against his grip and knew that it hadn't always been this way.

I can hear his voice again now as I struggle to wake up. The beach is no longer silent; even the boy has stopped crying. The sun has just come up over the horizon and is washing the dark sea red. It is going to be a beautiful day. I stumble out from behind the rock and see again that I am naked and still dripping wet. Once more I feel humiliated and shocked. On the concrete strip down to the sea a lifeboat has been beached and, further up, two police cars and an ambulance are parked. The cove seems to be full of dark-suited men and women walking up and down, staring at the sand. No one even notices me. A small group has gathered at the waves' edge and I can see Ali standing there, looking down at something lying by his feet. I shout his name but he doesn't turn. A policeman puts his arm around Alistair's shoulders. A dog barks and starts to run towards me, then stops and growls. Nobody looks up and when the dog's handler arrives, he pulls at the dog, ordering it to be still. I ask the handler if I can borrow his jacket but he ignores me, fussing around the dog. Alistair continues to look down into the water and then I realise what it is they have found. It was female. Her puffy flesh is white and when they turn her over they gasp in horror, for something has been eating away at her face.

Then I can see that it is me, my naked body there in the water; my eyes gone, my hair dull, lank and plastered to my head. I look down at my body's naked feet, several toes of which are missing; then I look down at my other naked feet and see that they have not left a single footprint in the sand.

'Yes, it is my wife.' says Ali and looks up. At me. His eyes grow wide as he sees me and his face changes to the colour of winter skies. Then I remember him in the bathroom, his bitter smile and his strong, strong hands at my throat. I remember hearing my voice begging him and the merciless pressure in my chest.

'What's this?' I ask and Ali cries out while all the other men continue to stand staring at the body on the sand. 'You're a fool, Alistair, bringing me here. Eventually someone will think to tell the police that I couldn't have been skinny-dipping. I hated the sea, hated it so much I never learned to swim.'

From across the strand I hear the boy starting to sob again, but this time it's my name he's crying, 'Helen, Helen, where are you? I am so frightened here all on my own.' And only I can hear his dead voice calling.

RUBY RED, DIAMOND WHITE

Debbie Moon

I'm still not sure why I took up with Darren. Now he's gone, I'm finding it hard to think of anything that I found attractive about him. Mostly, I suppose, I agreed to date him because of the things he wasn't.

He wasn't a smoker – he always said the smell hung on a suit for months – and he wasn't unemployed, and he wasn't on parole. Round here, that practically makes you Brad Pitt.

The one thing that should have been a plus turned out to be his downfall, and that was his wardrobe. Everything in it was designer – real designer, not ten-quid-down-the-market designer. His sister worked for a fashion mag and got him all the leftover gear from photoshoots half price after they'd done with it. It didn't always fit, but Darren wore it anyway.

So there I was, on the arm of the smartest guy in Bury. In fact, I spent more time on his sofa than his arm – because even at half price, most of his wages from the Post Office were going on clothes, and that meant that we couldn't go out much. I mean, you can't go down the burger bar in a Gucci suit, can you? You'd never get the grease out.

Every couple of weeks, we'd scrape together the money to go to a restaurant, or to cover the entry fee to a club in town. We couldn't afford to drink once we were in the club, or buy anything but the set meal, but Darren could sit and talk loudly about how he was 'up and coming' and anyone who got in his way would be sorry, and I could enjoy the dance music and check out what the other women were wearing.

Which brings me to the other problem with going out with Darren. I was definitely not allowed to let the side down.

I was strictly forbidden to wear the same dress twice, and I always had to dress to 'coordinate' with him. No low-cut tops, no sequins or shiny fabrics. 'You look like a tin of Quality Street,' he'd say, like that made any sense. Green was too vibrant, red too tarty. Patterns were definitely out.

In fact, the only colour Darren really liked me to wear was black. I wore every Little Black Dress in my wardrobe, my mum's wardrobe, my sister's and my friends'. By December, I only had two cousins and the receptionist at work left to borrow from. I figured it had been nearly a year by then, so maybe I could start rotating through all the dresses again and he wouldn't notice.

Then Darren's sister sent him the invitation.

'Champagne Gala!' Darren said, waving the gold-edged invitation in my face as I came through the door clutching the takeaway and a pile of junk mail. 'In the Harriot Hotel Ballroom, Mayfair. Us and a hundred top-notch designers, the crème de la crème. This is my chance, Katy, babe. This is my chance to impress the people who really matter.'

'Impress them?' I asked, dumping everything on top of the washing-up he'd promised he'd do before I got home. 'Impress them with what?'

Darren looked at me like I was daft. 'My drive, babe. My energy. My *ideas*.'

The most original idea I could remember Darren having was topping a pizza with pickled onions, and I couldn't see all those fancy West End types being interested in a soggy pizza that made your breath smell. But he looked happy, and he had his hand in the air for another can of Diamond White, so I just threw him one and left him to it.

'I'll wear the grey Mao jacket,' he announced to no one in particular. 'And the cream shirt – no, the white... God, I need to think about this.' Can in hand, he headed for the bedroom. 'Do you think the tan shoes, or the brown?'

I didn't answer. He didn't usually notice anyway.

I was putting his share of the chicken tikka masala in the microwave for later when Darren stuck his head round the door again. 'And don't you plan anything for Saturday. We're going shopping.'

Yeah, I know what you're thinking. A bloke who looks forward to taking you dress shopping?

But you've never been shopping with Darren.

Forty-seven shops in two towns. No lunch – 'lunch is for wimps!' – no coffee, and strictly no offering an opinion. Even the shop assistants couldn't get a word in. Darren was the expert, and he was going to find me the perfect dress if it killed me.

We tried short and long, sleeveless and sleeved. Ballgowns were too formal; cocktail dresses were too 'average'. Frills made my hips look big and collars made my neck look short. And absolutely everything he made me try on was designed for Barbie.

By the end of the day I didn't feel like a person at all. I felt like a grab bag of random body parts that hadn't been designed to go together, none of which fitted all these lovely dresses designed for the way a woman 'should' look.

Finally, at three minutes past closing time and with all the staff grinding their teeth and looking meaningfully at their watches, Darren pronounced the clingy black taffeta dress that I was wearing 'absolutely perfect'.

'I look like an elephant in a stretch bandage,' I told him. 'An elephant in mourning, at that.'

'You've got a week to drop a few pounds.'

I turned round and looked at my rear end in the mirror. There was barely room for it all. 'Darren, the only way I'd actually fit into this dress is to have liposuction.'

He looked at me for a moment, and then shook his head. 'Don't be daft, babe. There's no way we can afford that.' He waved his hand at the assistant, like he'd seen someone do in a movie the other night. 'We'll take it. Pay the girl, babe, we need to be home in time for Celebrity Fashion Disasters...'

That night, while Darren was snoring and probably dreaming of his glittering career as a fashion guru, I stood in the hallway with that stupid, flimsy, jet-black dress in one hand and my maxed-out credit card in the other, and I cried.

I should have left him. I would have left him. But as I stood there weeping all over the two yards of crepe that had just cost me six months salary, I suddenly had this feeling that I was about to get my revenge. Darren had finally gone too far, and the slow wheels of fate were grinding their way round to him. All I had to do was wait.

The shoes were in the charity shop down the street from the office.

Good thing too. I'd never have even looked at them if they'd been in a real shoe shop. I'd already started making my own sandwiches and economising on takeaway coffee, like that was going to make a significant dent in my next credit card bill.

I don't think I'd ever taken much notice of the shop before. Usually all they have on display are sensible winter coats, and tatty paperbacks with plane crashes on the cover. But it was still open when I left work, which it usually isn't, and with it just getting dark, the shoes stood out in the lit window like they were on a stage.

They were red. Huge stiletto heels, twinkly like the glitter you used to put on home-made Christmas cards as a kid, and they had this silver buckle on the toe even though they didn't need buckling up. They were what you dream grown-up shoes are like when you're five. They were perfect. They were me!

Standing there staring in at them, my mouth wide open, I could finally see a way of wearing that stupid dress without feeling like a comedy act.

And Darren was going to hate them with every fibre of his being.

So, of course, I rushed inside and bought them.

By the time I got home, Darren was on his third can of Diamond White, and sort of jittery and hyperactive, like Mabel at work gets when she doesn't have her fag break.

'You're late!' He yelled, throwing the can at the wall as I came in. 'I told you, we need to dye your hair tonight, or it won't—'

I opened the bag and lifted out the red shoes.

'I'm not dying my hair. I like my hair brown. And I'm wearing these to your precious ball, so get used to it.'

Darren looked at the shoes like they were made out of dead babies or something. Honestly. Like they disgusted him.

'Is that what you want people to think of you?'

'Darren, I don't much care what people think of—'

He was already halfway across the room towards me, weaving like a drunk, and for the first time I was actually scared of him. 'You want them to think you're some silly girl who wears fake fur down the Roxy Club, and drinks cocktails, and laughs like a fishwife?'

'I like cocktails!'

And I don't much like you any more, I was thinking. And that was when Darren snatched the shoes out of my hand and started trying to stuff his size 11 feet – Italian cashmere socks and all – into them.

I should've stopped him. I mean, he was going to break them. But part of me wanted to see stuck-up Darren fall over in three inch heels – and actually, I think part of me knew what was going to happen and didn't want to get in the way.

After a moment's struggling, he managed to get his feet into them – which confirmed my feeling that these were no ordinary shoes – and starting mincing up and down behind the sofa.

'Look at me, I'm Katy! I've got no dress sense and big hips and I don't care what people think—'

It was weird, actually. For the first time ever, Darren was very nearly as tall as me.

'I'm a fairy princess in my stupid heels, oooh, let's go to Oz—'

He knocked his heels together once, twice, wobbled, went for the third time—

And as the sparkly heels of the red shoes touched together for the final time, Darren disappeared into thin air, leaving behind – the shoes and a faint smell of French cologne.

I took a day off today, so I could take the dress back. The assistant remembered me, and she was really nice about it. 'I know it's none of my business,' she said, while she was arranging the refund, 'but if I was you—'

'Ah, don't worry. Darren's had to go away for a while – and I won't exactly be counting the days until he comes back.'

Smiling, the assistant handed me back my credit card. 'Good girl. And by the way – love the shoes—'

On the way home, I stopped off and rented *The Wizard of Oz*. I felt I should reassure myself that Darren would be okay there. I feel a bit sorry for him. He's not exactly going to make friends, is he? He'll tell the Tin Man that he's too shiny, and the Cowardly Lion that fur is so last decade – and the Scarecrow, well…

I wear the shoes all the time now. They're so comfy, and sexy. James from Accounts has found an excuse to call in to my office four times since I started wearing them to work.

The problem is, I know my heels knocked together just by accident the other day, and I think it happened again today – and that only leaves one to go.

ED

✂

Eloise Williams

This is my green cardy. I call it Ed. People tell me it is strange to call your cardigan something. I don't care and that's a fact.

My mother says I am twenty-five now. She tells me all the time.

- Don't do that, you are twenty-five now.
- Don't say that, you are twenty-five now.
- Don't look like that, you are twenty-five now.

I just stay quiet, but I think I don't know how to look any different. I can't really change my face.

My green cardy is my favourite thing in the world because it is mine and I chose it and I didn't choose any of my other clothes. Usually my mum or my nana bring me clothes that they have bought for me, and they are all like, pink, with pictures of puppies or cats, and I think I am not twelve anymore.

My green cardy is nine years old and smells of grass when it has soaked up the sun; it reminds me of being in a tent when the rain starts falling lightly in the spring. I sleep with it under my pillow now, in case they throw it out 'cos it's missing a button, has a hole in the arm and is

  - way too tight
    Or, as I like to call it, *cwtchy*.

My name is Eleri, which either means unknown, or people don't know what it means when you look it up in a dictionary. It is sad that Eleri rhymes with scary. This gives all the people who

  - don't know better
    a really easy way to make me angry.

I had a banana sandwich before we set off, and I had toast with eggs this morning. Sometimes I have toast with jam, but that's usually on a Thursday when I get up later to rest after my Wednesday outing. Today is Wednesday. Today my friend takes me out. His name is Mikey, and he is cool, and lets me do pretty much anything I want

  - within reason.

He is the only man I have seen who wears a scarf on his head, and has ribbons on his bag which are sun yellow and sky blue, which makes it easy to spot him in a crowd.
  The walk is four miles, he tells me, so I wear my walking shoes.

Mum makes a fuss before we leave about it being

- too far
- too dangerous
- too everything,

this just means I want to go more.

Mikey ties Ed around my waist and we set off into the forest of trees. The ground beneath my feet is crunchy and stumbly, and my balance isn't good like other people's. I've got a scab on my knee from where I fell over the other day, so I have a big plaster which makes my friends ooh and aah, and that is good. We see a butterfly flutter by, and Mikey whistles a song which sounds like something from a telly commercial, and I sing along like lalalalala. Even though I never heard it before I sound pretty brilliant.

We are walking to the waterfall today. Mikey showed me pictures of it in a photograph book and I wanted to go there right away, but that was not our going out day so I couldn't. We've been planning it for three days. I looked at a map and copied it onto paper for us. He got us two walking sticks off a tree out the back garden and put bells on them. They jingle, jangle, tinkle as we walk, though I've given mine to Mikey 'cos it's too much like hard work and that's for sure.

The waterfall we are walking to is called 'Sgwd yr Eira', which means 'Falls of Snow', which doesn't make hardly any sense at all until you see a picture. You can walk behind it. I never heard of any waterfall you can walk behind in real life before, and so that's why we are on our way.

I've got water in a bottle round my neck and I keep sipping some even though it tastes of plastic. The sun is big. Like a giant gold coin and I can't look at it for squinting, and Mikey says I'll get crow's feet, which makes no sense at all 'cos why would my feet change into a bird's because I look at the sun? He puts my glasses on me and the world becomes pink and shiny, and we walk some more.

And then we walk some more again.

I'm following the map with my finger, and on the red dotty line there is a river which I have put as three blue wavy lines, and we haven't even reached the river, and I think we are lost, and to be honest I'm a little bit fed up because this was meant to be an adventure not an endless trudgety trudgety trudge. Mikey is in front of me and his footsteps kick up dust in clouds and puffs. I scuff my own shoes for a bit, listening to their sound as it matches my heartbeat, and then I cough a lot to make a point about his walking habits and to get a break. We sit and I cough some more, like a lady that I saw on *Casualty*, and I try to get some blood up but there is none to come. When that doesn't get me much attention I start to cry. This is a certain sure way to get a hug, and to go back to the car and go to get some chips.

'What's up, kiddo?' Mikey sits down next to me which I usually like but he smells of hot and his skin is wet.

'I am not a kiddo.' This is a sure for certain sign to him that I am in a strop.

'You're not giving up on me already are you, my intrepid explorer?' He smiles his big white teeth smile and I catch a spark of gold in his mouth, like buried treasure and it makes me think of pirates and how they were brave, and I don't know what intrepid means but I think he is calling me a scaredy cat.

'My knee hurts.' It doesn't but I need a reason to be cross.

'Let me see.' Mikey takes off the plaster and it leaves a black square where the dirt has stuck around the edges, and my skin is very bluey where the plaster was. He tuts a bit and shakes his head. 'Do you want to go on? Or shall we take you to the hospital?'

A bee buzzes past, and he is lucky I don't bat it into his eye.

'I never said I wanted to go back.' I am stubborn

- at the best of times.

We have been walking for a hundred and fifty years now. Mikey has pointed to lots of mountains that all look the same. He keeps showing me flowers though which are nice colours like lemon and lilac and candyfloss pink, and for a while we play 'he loves me, he loves me not' which is strange for both of us cos Mikey is a boy and I don't have a boyfriend.

I had a boyfriend once at music club but that was

- not allowed,

so now I just have boys who are friends and the difference is we don't hold hands, unless it is for a game like drama.

'Listen.' Mikey puts his hand on my shoulder and I let him put it there 'cos he is safe. The wind makes a sound like a moan, then a whine, then a rush and I turn around quickly as I'm sure that a tidal wave is on its way to smash me into smithereens.

Smithereens is a good word. I've smashed lots of things into smithereens. Mirrors, plates, cups, mum's photo frame, mum's glasses, the shower door, part of the car, the shed window, that kind of thing. I listen with my ear to the sound and my hair splashing across the front of my face in waves. Mikey's face has lit up like an electric bulb, and he is saying excited things like 'wicked' and 'awesome', and I copy him because it makes him happy, and he is good to me and he has the money for chips.

The wind blasts past us with a smash and a crack and is gone.

It excited Mikey so much he wants to walk a bit more quickly, and I try my best even though I am not

- nimble
  or
- dainty
  and I'm
- certainly not going to be a ballerina.

I drink my last bit of plasticy water down and I am just beginning to get really super mad when we come to the edge of the world, and Mikey points down and through the trees you can see it.

Now when I said you could understand the name 'Falls of Snow' from the picture, I believed it and that's for certain sure, but looking at it now I know that you could never understand it till you seen it with your own

- baby blues.

Me and Mikey and Ed hug and jump up and down a bit, only

I jump a bit less 'cos my feet are sore.

'And now for the ultimate challenge,' Mikey points at a million steps down and I think that he is wrong 'cos the ultimate challenge will be climbing back up, but the water is so beautiful and looks frothy, diamondy, and glittery like Christmas and magicy like fairies, and I haven't got any plasticy water left so we go.

'Mum was right,' we are halfway down and I am crying, not to get a cuddle but just 'cos I can't stop.

Mikey sits down next to me and smiles. He is always bloody smiling.

'Your mum is right about a lot of things, Eleri, but not this. This is your time to prove to her that you are a grown-up. Show her that you can do things for yourself. I promise you it'll be worth the struggle if you make it.'

And his voice is so soft it is like a pillow on my head, and I look up at the steps behind us and see how very far I have come already and I know that he is right, it is kind of now or never, I can't be like this for always.

'You aren't Barack Obama, you know,' I say, because I am always sarcastic when he makes a speech even when he is saying the right things, and I am very well up on current affairs. Ed squeezes me extra hard around my waist and I use him to wipe the tears from my eyes, and the snot from my nose, which he is used to 'cos he is my oldest friend apart from Mum.

I could tell you about the rest of the steps, and how I banged my knee and gashed my legs till blood ran red into my sock, and how we had to walk sideways on the rocks holding hands 'cos it was high up and slippery, soaking and silly dangerous, but you would be scared and I want to tell you about the waterfall.

Shut your eyes and think of white. And then think of that white falling in front of you, like a curtain of heavy thick snowflakes, and then specks of that white landing on your face like tiny giggles or kisses. Imagine a noise in your ears, like a train rattling through a tunnel, or a million people playing drums, or everyone in the world jumping up and down all at once. Think what you imagine heaven to look like, and then make it better and louder by a hundred, and take out the harps.

I look at Mikey, and his face is shining like a lamp, and his eyes are on fire they are so bright, and his mouth is in the shape that a mouth makes when there is a whooooooo hooooo coming out, but I can't hear it because the water is filling my ears with its own happy shouts.

I take a step back as some big splashes hit my face with an ice-cold slap that would wake up a hibernating hedgehog, and step on something soft.

And there he is. Ed. My oldest friend. He has loosened himself from around my middle where he usually cuddles, and is lying in a pool as clear as the shiniest, cleanest mirror.

People think I'm strange. Most people don't understand their clothes like I do, but then most people really don't listen.

We come to an understanding without speaking, Ed and I. This is our time. This is our moment to be free. This is the time we will grow up, and we will take on the world on our own, and not cow down to the bullies, and not let Mum tell us what we have to do, or where we have to go, or that we

- aren't strong enough

or
- clever enough
or
- brave enough

and sometimes we'll have eggs on a Thursday too, if we want them.

I pick Ed up and I am shaking. Partly with the cold and partly because I am excited and afraid, but in a good way. Ed drips tears down my arm, but they are happy tears. Mikey gives me a little nod, though he looks serious as hell. I hold Ed to my face, but just for a second 'cos he already smells different, and soon we will be strangers. We don't need to speak our goodbyes 'cos we know.

Ed flies when I throw him, through the fall of snow to the wide open world. I see him in jigsaw bits and pieces through the always-changing white. He swims hard in bubbles and gurgles, the sun catching him as he bounces off rocks in bright meadow green. And then he is gone, all the way to the sea.

I salute. I don't know why I salute; it just feels right. I suppose I feel like the captain for a change, and even though there are a hundred and fifty million steps to go straight up, and about a hundred and twenty miles to get to the car, I can't wipe the grin off my face, and I'm sure that Ed can't either.

EDITOR AND AUTHOR BIOGRAPHIES

Yasmin Ali grew up reading the fashion trade press at her parents' womenswear shop and celebrated her 10th birthday by demanding an Yves St Laurent trouser suit! Although most of her career has been in teaching, training and consultancy, Yasmin has retained an interest in fashion and from 2002 has edited a fashion website. Yasmin has written a number of articles and chapters in non-fiction books and journals, as well as contributing to the Honno crime fiction anthology *Written in Blood*.

Lindsay Ashford is a former BBC journalist and the author of five crime novels. Her second, *Strange Blood*, was shortlisted for the Theakston's Old Peculier Crime Novel of the Year Award and she is now published in the USA, Canada and Brazil as well as the UK. She has co-edited two Honno anthologies, *Strange Days Indeed* and *Written In Blood*, and her short stories have appeared in several of Honno's previous collections. One of these, *Passion Fruit*, was broadcast on BBC Radio 4. Originally from the West Midlands, she now lives on the west coast of Wales near Aberystwyth.

Hilary Bowers is a sixty-year-old divorcee. Yorkshire born and bred, she lived for twenty years in the environs of the beautiful coastal university town of Aberystwyth. She is the deputy manager of Barnado's charity shop, a novice bell-ringer, enthusiastic newcomer to outdoor bowls, a member of Wells Little Theatre and has recently started training with the St. John Ambulance Brigade. A novelist by inclination, she also enjoys writing short stories, two of which have been published in previous Honno fiction anthologies; *Coming up Roses* and *Written in Blood*.

Suzy Ceulan Hughes was born in England but has lived in Wales since 1977. She is a writer, translator and book reviewer. 'A Woman of Grace' is her second short story to be published. Her first, 'Broken Words', was one of the winning stories in the Jane Austen Short Story Award, 2009 and is included in the award anthology, *Dancing with Mr Darcy*.

Sue Coffey is from the Cynon Valley and now lives in the Vale of Glamorgan. She lived in Gwent and Cyprus in intervening decades. She works for a training association and, until recently, was a tutor on the Learn programme at Cardiff University. She has an MA in Creative Writing from Swansea University and has had stories published in national magazines and Honno anthologies. Her work has been shortlisted for a Legend Award and the Bristol Short Story Prize. Happily settled at last, her ambition is to produce a publishable collection of short stories. She'd also like to become known as the village's eccentric 'writer-in-residence'.

Alys Conran Born and brought up in Bangor, Alys studied literature in Scotland and Barcelona, graduating at Edinburgh with a first class MA before returning to north Wales. She currently lives and writes in Bethesda and works with children and young people on Ynys Mon.

Hilary Cooper has eight-year-old twins who take great delight in announcing to mortified acquaintances that they were *'made in Wales – on the bank of the River Twymyn'*. Seeing as the secret is out, she may as well also admit to their Welsh middle names (Cerys and Ceinwen) and her enduring love for the place that spawned them. Since then, a restless husband has meant several moves and a lot of adapting. Currently a houseparent in a boarding school, her extended family includes twenty Chinese boys who love her because she washes sweaty sports kit at 11pm, and a big, smelly dog called Kendra who loves her regardless.

Sue Fortune is a Welsh woman who has lived in interesting times. She leads an outwardly innocuous existence with her dogs, bees and hens in a village in north-east Wales. 'The White Sandals' is her first published fiction.

Daisy Golding is a pseudonym. The writer has lived in Wales for ten years after twenty or so in London and more before that in the Midlands. This is her first piece of fiction since school.

Carys Green was born in London and studied Law at UCW Aberystwyth before training as a journalist at the London College of Printing. Her work has featured in numerous publications and she has read her poetry on BBC Radio Wales. She lives in St. Dogmael's, Pembrokeshire and is currently working on her first novel.

Christine Harrison Born and brought up on the Isle of Wight, Christine has lived in Wales now for over thirty years. She has been writing short stories consistently, drawn to the form early on. One or two have won national prizes, notably the *Cosmopolitan* prize – this story later collected by Serpent's Tail in *The Best of Cosmopolitan*. Lately she has turned to the historical novel.

Jenny Henn is a Christian Welsh speaker from Cwm, Blaenau Gwent. Her proudest moment was receiving the short story trophy at the National Eisteddfod in Cardiff 2008. She likes wild weather and hates beetroot.

Lorraine Jenkin wrote *Chocolate Mousse and Two Spoons* whilst walking around the wilds of South America with a tent and a toothbrush. *Eating Blackbirds* was written in the corners of playgroups and whilst sitting in lay-bys with two small children sleeping in the back of the car. Her third novel is being written whilst searching for lost shoes and PE kits, and battling with all-day morning sickness with her third child. But then, life was never meant to be easy... Lorraine also writes articles for publications including *The Times*, the *Guardian* and the *Observer*, as well as blogging at www.lorrainejenkin. blosgspot.com. Her style has been described by Bookbag as being "gloriously off-the-wall...". Lorraine lives in Mid Wales with her partner Huw.

Rebecca Lees is a journalist. Formerly a staff reporter at the *South Wales Echo*, she now freelances for the *BBC, MSN, Media Wales, Metro* and many more. 'Reunion' is her first piece of published fiction. Originally from Swansea, Rebecca lives near Pontypridd with her two small children and is valiantly learning Welsh in an attempt to keep up with their annoyingly effortless bilingualism.

Jo Lloyd was the winner of the 2009 Asham Short Story Award (*Waving at the Gardener*, Bloomsbury) and of the 2009 Willesden International Herald Short Story Prize (*New Short Stories 3*, Pretend Genius Press). She was brought up in South Wales and is currently living in Oxford.

Jean Lyon lives in North Wales and has had academic writing published as articles, chapters and a book, *Becoming Bilingual*. This was based on her research into the bilingual language development of children in Ynys Mon and was published by Multilingual Matters. She has had a number of stories published, including one in an earlier Honno anthology, and writes poetry. Her main interest is her characters' self-awareness, and she has written a novel on this theme.

Barbara McGaughey was raised and educated in South Wales. She spent the first few years of her career teaching English in London and abroad. She returned to South Wales in the late 1960s and now lives in Swansea. She has a daughter, a son and three grandsons.

Debbie Moon is an author and screenwriter based in mid-Wales. Her short stories have been published in the UK, the US and further afield, and her first novel, *Falling*, was longlisted for the Welsh Book Of The Year Award. She is also developing ideas for a number of television and film companies, including a children's series, a science fiction thriller, and a drama about Dr Barnardo.

Joanna Piesse writes short stories and plays. She has lived mainly in Norwich, London and Tyneside. Falling in love with a Geordie provided her with three stepchildren and she recently became a mum. Joanna believes bicycles should have right of way over cars.

Claudia Rapport moved from Paris to Cardiff where she has been living with her husband for over thirty years. A teacher of both French and English for over three decades she completed an MA in creative writing six years ago and enjoyed helping other writers when running classes for the Life Long Learning Department at Cardiff University. Her work has been published by *Cambrensis* and the *New Welsh Review*, has been shortlisted for several competitions including; Frome, *Writers' News*, Short Story Wales and *Mslexia*, and she has contributed to a previous Honno anthology.
She is working on a novel and putting 'consular' anecdotes together in the form of a book.

Rin Simpson is editor of the *Western Mail*'s women's supplement, *WM*, and fashion editor of *WM* magazine. Raised in Cape Town, South Africa, she moved to England with her mum and sister in 1994, but hadn't visited Wales before she applied to study journalism at Cardiff University in 2004. Rin has written short stories since she could hold a pencil (the first one being an illustrated tale following the adventures of Tommy the tadpole) but this is the first time her fiction has appeared in print. She is now determined to get to work on a full-length novel – and finish it this time!

Kerry Steed travels around Britain and the world working as an actor and musician. Recently, she took a break from the road and started writing in a shed at the bottom of a garden in Pembrokeshire; she would like to do more of this. 'I am Wearing no Make-up' is her first short story and her first published work. Thank you to all her friends who have given her floor space!

Sarah Todd Taylor moved from Yorkshire to Ceredigion at the age of eight. She graduated from the University of Wales, Aberystwyth in 1998 with a PhD in early modern ballads. Her short stories have featured in three of Honno's previous anthologies and she continues to work towards finishing a larger work of fiction for children. She lives in Aberystwyth with a long-suffering husband and a succession of adorable hamsters.

Stephanie Tillotson (editor) joined the BBC in 1989 and worked in television and radio for many years before moving to the independent sector in Wales. For the past ten years she has been teaching, directing and performing for the theatre and is also a published playwright. Originally from Gilwern near Abergavenny, Stephanie now lives in Aberystwyth where, until recently, she was teaching in the Department of Theatre, Film and Television Studies at the university. She is now studying at the Shakespeare Institute, University of Birmingham, where she is specialising in Theatre and Performance. This is the first time that Stephanie has edited for Honno though she has been published by them several times, most recently in *Dancing with Mr Darcy*.

Eloise Williams Born and raised in South Wales, Eloise has worked in theatre for the past ten years and much of her writing is informed by her drama work for people with special needs. In addition to her short stories she writes plays for Wales-based companies and her poetry has brought her success in the Marches Literary Prize, the Welsh Poetry competition, Leaf Books' poetry competition and *Undercurrents*. She is currently studying for an MA in Creative and Media Writing at Swansea University.

MORE FROM HONNO

Short stories Classics Autobiography Fiction

Founded in 1986 to publish the best of women's writing,
Honno publishes a wide range of titles from Welsh women.

Praise for Honno's books:

"a marvellous compilation of reminiscences"
Time Out

"A cracking good read"
dovegreyreader.co.uk

*"Illuminating, poignant, entertaining
and unputdownable"*
The Big Issue

ABOUT HONNO

Honno Welsh Women's Press was set up in 1986 by a group of women who felt strongly that women in Wales needed wider opportunities to see their writing in print and to become involved in the publishing process. Our aim is to develop the writing talents of women in Wales, give them new and exciting opportunities to see their work published and often to give them their first 'break' as a writer.

Honno is registered as a community co-operative. Any profit that Honno makes is invested in the publishing programme. Women from Wales and around the world have expressed their support for Honno by buying shares. Supporters liability is limited to the amount invested and each supporter has a vote at the Annual General Meeting.

To buy shares or to receive further information about forthcoming publications, please write to Honno at the address below, or visit our website: www.honno.co.uk.

Honno
Unit 14, Creative Units
Aberystwyth Arts Centre
Penglais Campus,
Aberystwyth
Ceredigion, SY23 3GL

All Honno titles can be ordered online at
www.honno.co.uk
or by sending a cheque to Honno.
Free p&p to all UK addresses